Maintenance Required

Maintenance Required

By

Rodney Riesel

Published by Island Holiday Publishing
East Greenbush, NY

Special thanks to:

Pamela Guerriere

Kevin Cook

Cover Image and Design by:

Connie Fitsik

To learn about my other books friend me at

https://www.facebook.com/rodneyriesel

For Brenda,
Kayleigh, Ethan
& Peyton

Chapter One

"Ya know, trouble really has a way of finding you," said Detective Rance.

I sat in a creaky old wooden chair next to his gray metal desk in the Fernandina Police Department. I sipped my can of Diet Coke and shrugged my shoulders.

Calvin Rance, forty-two years old, had been with the department for twenty years and was now Fernandina Beach's only plainclothes detective. He was a tall man, around six-two, and had a wiry but muscular build. His blond hair was cut short like a new recruit in basic training. I had only recently met Calvin and had never seen him outside of a police investigation. So as far as I knew, he always wore a white, short-sleeved, button-up shirt, light gray slacks, and a matching sport coat. And one could spot his black leather Chuck Taylor high-tops from a mile away.

"Ya know what I mean?" asked Rance. He looked up from his computer screen and waited for my answer.

I shrugged again and cocked my head a little.

"That's all you got for me? he asked. "A shrug?"

"I don't know what you want me to say," I replied.

Rance shook his head and returned his attention to his monitor. "I guess I don't know either," he grumbled.

I started to shrug yet again, but caught myself. I looked around the squad room as Rance typed with one finger. A uniformed officer who lived near me, and I kind of knew, nodded and smiled as he walked by. I nodded back. W*hat's his name?* I thought. *Bob? Bill? Rob? I don't know.*

"You're how old?" Rance asked.

"Forty-eight," I replied.

"Eyes?"

"Two."

I grinned to show I was joking. Rance didn't look up. His typing finger hovered expectantly over the keyboard.

"Color?" he snapped.

"Green."

He looked up at me. "Red hair," he commented.

"I prefer to think of it as strawberry blond."

"Address?"

"2102 Taurus Court."

"Married?"

"Yup."

"You say you heard a noise and got out of bed?"

"No. Like I already said, I was sleeping on the couch. I heard a noise, and when I opened my eyes, I see some guy coming through my living room window."

Rance stared at me for a second. "Why were you sleeping on the couch?"

"Is that relevant?"

"No, but it just made me think: you must irritate your wife as much as you irritate me. I'm thinking she kicked you out of the bedroom."

"If you must know, she wasn't home from work yet, and I just fell asleep on the couch watching a movie."

"Where does she work?"

"She's a waitress over at Brett's Waterway Cafe." Rance wasn't typing, so I knew none of the latest questions had anything to do with what had happened last night in my living room; he was just being nosy.

He leaned forward with his corded forearms propped on the edge of the desk. "And you work part-time at Collins' Hardware as a maintenance man."

"Yup."

Rance leaned back in his chair again. He ruminated like a cow chewing its cud. "Tell me something, Mr. Langley," he said slowly and insinuatingly, "how does a part-time waitress and a part-time maintenance man make enough money to live in a house on Taurus Court?" He leaned forward again. There was a "gotcha" expression on his face.

I knew there was no need for me to answer half of Rance's questions, but I didn't have anything else to do. My wife, Gayle, was working until three, and I didn't work Fridays—or Mondays, for that matter.

"Well," I said, in response to his latest question, "we're both retired."

"Retired?" Rance asked. "Retired from what?"

"Gayle is retired from the military—the Navy. She retired a little over five years ago."

"And you?"

"I used to own a construction business. I sold it about a year ago, and got the job at the hardware store."

Rance nodded his head. "Huh." He stabbed a few more keys on his keyboard. "So you see this guy coming through the window. Did he see you?"

"No. The movie I had been watching ended after I fell asleep, and the TV screen was dark. The only light on in the house was a little light over the kitchen sink, so the room was pretty dark as well."

"But you saw him?"

"Yup."

"But he couldn't see you?"

"I imagine he could have … if I made as much noise as he did coming through the window."

"Where was your revolver at the time?"

"It was on a shelf in the closet in my bedroom, in a lockbox."

"And the perp never heard you as you retrieved it?"

"I'm pretty light on my feet," I explained. "I used to be a dancer."

Rance cocked his head like a Yorkie hearing the word treat. "Seriously?" he asked.

"No," I replied. "I waited for the guy to walk into the kitchen and got up as quietly as I could. I went into the bedroom to get my gun. When I came back down the hallway, he was standing there with a knife in his hand, so I shot him in the leg."

"And then?"

"And then he screamed, 'You shot me!'"

"Did you say anything to him?"

"Yes."

"What?"

"I said, 'Yeah, I know, and if you don't drop that knife, I'll shoot you again.'"

"But he dropped the knife?"

"Yup. I guess he wasn't as stupid as he looked."

Rance leaned back in his chair again and interlocked his fingers behind his head. "Mr. Langley, do you—"

"Just call me Rex," I said.

"Okay. *Rex*, do you feel you had any option other than shooting Mr. Haskell in the leg?"

"Well, yes. I could have shot him in the head."

"That's not what I mean, *Rex*."

I didn't really like the way Rance kept pronouncing my name. He said it the same way he would have if I had told him my name was Spot or Rover. "I know that's not what you mean, *Rance.*" Two can play that game. "But that's my answer."

Rance shifted his weight forward in the chair and unclasped his hands. His magic finger hit about fifteen more keys on the keyboard and said, "I think I have everything I need."

I downed the rest of my soft drink and held up the can. "What would you like me to do with this?"

The look on Rance's face said he wanted to tell me where I could stick it. "Just leave it there on the desk."

"So that's it?" I asked.

"For now," he replied. "Will you be at the hardware store later this afternoon, if I have any more questions?"

"Nope." I replied. "I don't work on Fridays."

"Must be nice."

"I don't work on Mondays either." Might as well pour salt in the wound.

"I have your number if I need you."

"Yup," I said, and escorted myself out of the station.

Chapter Two

I walked out the front door of the police station and jumped into my old Ford pickup—a '94 F-150. I bought the old girl about three years ago and had her completely restored. First I had the engine rebuilt. Then I had her painted and had four new tires and rims slapped on her. A year after I got her, she looked like she had just rolled off a Detroit assembly line. I didn't do any of the work myself, of course, because the only thing I know how to do when it comes to automobile repair is putting air in the tires. Anything else I need done gets done by a certified mechanic … except oil changes; Gayle does that. Yeah, it's a little embarrassing to have your wife lying under a vehicle in the driveway, but hey, I do crouch down beside her and hand her the tools she needs. I can build an entire house with a hammer, saw, and a level, but the mechanics of a combustible engine are beyond me.

I made the ten minute trip from the station to our house and pulled into the driveway. When I got inside I soaked the dishes from the night before, and then threw a load of my own laundry into the washing machine. I started doing my own laundry soon after I retired. I figured it was one less thing Gayle would have to do. Back when I took over my own laundry, I tried to do Gayle's laundry as well, but that didn't go over too well. In the first three loads I ruined one sweater, three tops, and one pair of white jeans. Evidently there was a brand new red T-shirt of mine in the load. Oh well, live and learn. She went back to doing her own laundry after that.

After I got the washing machine going, I swept the kitchen and vacuumed the living room. About four years ago a door-to-door salesman had talked Gayle into buying a pricey Kirby vacuum with a gazillion bells and whistles. After the in-home demonstration—and here I thought that kind of thing went out with *Leave It To Beaver*—Gayle was a believer. The machine still works like brand new, but its shampoo system hadn't been a match for Delbert Haskell's bloodstain near the end of the hall. It was still there, even after both Gayle and I had each given it a good going-over with the Kirby.

When I finished vacuuming, I returned to the kitchen and washed the dishes. I left them on the counter to air dry.

I made myself a cup of coffee, turned on the television, put my feet up on the coffee table, and let out a long sigh. *I wonder if I should rent a steam cleaner and try to get the blood stain out*, I thought, *or should I just go ahead and have the carpeting replaced.* Then I remembered seeing a quirky indie movie called Sunshine Cleaning on cable, about two clueless hotties that go into the crime-scene cleanup biz. For the next minute or so, I daydreamed about Emily Blunt and Amy Adams on their hands and knees scrubbing my carpet.

Laying carpet was something else I didn't do. Sure, I had laid carpet in a few rooms in apartments over the hardware store, but that was cheap carpeting that some tenant was just going to ruin in two years anyway. When I laid carpet in the apartments, I just cut it to size and stapled the edges. I want my carpet done right, so I'll hire a professional.

The living room and hall have the same carpeting, so we'll have to have the whole thing replaced. I wondered what our deductible was, and if gunshots to the leg were even covered. I returned my attention to the TV. Gayle would have the answers to all of my homeowner's insurance questions when she got home from work. She handles most of that stuff.

I watched *The Price Is Right* and then switched over to *The Jerry Springer Show*. I noticed I didn't hear the washing machine running anymore, so I went into the laundry room to throw my wet clothes into the dryer.

I considered myself one hell of a housekeeper. To my friends, I jokingly referred to myself as a stay-at-home dad. They usually remind me that our son moved out of the house over three years ago. To that I reply, "I'm a dad, I stay at home, I'm a stay-at-home dad." This was usually met with laughter. Two of my close friends—Paul Farber and Billy Hempstead—

call me Gayle's house bitch. I think I like *stay-at-home dad* much better.

I returned to the couch and sipped my coffee. Jerry Springer was interviewing a woman who used to be a man and was now cheating on her boyfriend with her boyfriend's wife. The wife just called the girlfriend a whore. *Oh no she di'int*, I thought.

My cell phone rang and I glanced at the screen. It was Kevin Collins, the owner of Collins' Hardware.

"Rex?" Kevin asked.

"Yeah?"

"Hey, uh, one of the tenants upstairs just called and said her bathtub faucet is leaking pretty bad."

"Who is it?" I asked.

"Maude Phelps, in twenty-one."

"She hasn't taken a bath in years," I deadpanned.

Kevin laughed. "I know, right?"

"You say it's leaking bad?"

"Pretty bad."

I looked at the time on my cell phone. *I wonder if I can run over there, fix the faucet, and be back before Days of Our Lives starts,* I thought. *Probably, if everything goes right.* "I'll be there in ten minutes," I said.

"Thanks," Kevin replied.

I hung up the cell and went into the bedroom— hopping over the bloodstain—to put on my work clothes.

On my way to the hardware store I called the hospital to see how Delbert Haskell—the guy I shot in the leg—was doing.

"Are you a relative?" the nurse asked.

"No," I replied. "I'm the guy who shot him. I just wanted to make sure he was doing okay."

"You're who?"

I knew I shouldn't have told her that the second I said it, but I repeated it any way. "The guy who shot him."

"Can I have your name, please?"

"Never mind," I said, and hung up.

Chapter Three

I pulled to the curb on Centre Street, in front of Amelia Island Coffee. I thought about going in and grabbing a cup to go, but I knew I was on a tight schedule. After all, my soap opera was starting at one.

I climbed out of my truck and opened my toolbox. I took out my tool belt, and my plumbing box, and carried them inside the hardware store.

Christine Collins was behind the checkout counter. "Hey, Rex," she said.

"Hey Chris," I replied.

"Did Kevin call you?" she asked.

"Yup. Apartment twenty-one?"

"Yeah," she said with a grin. "Old Maude."

"Can you call up there and let her know I'll be up in a second?"

Christine pulled a small, yellow, plastic box out from under the counter. She opened the top and walked her fingers through the index cards inside. When she got to Maude's card she pulled it out, read the phone number, and made the call. "Maude? It's Christine. Fine. You? Good. Rex is coming up in a few minutes to fix the faucet. Okay. Bye."

Christine hung up the phone and said, "She'll be waiting for you."

"Lucky me," I said, and walked out the front door.

There's an entrance to a stairway to the left of the hardware store entrance. The stairway goes to all three floors above the store. There's also another door on the right side of the building, off the alley. This door leads to a hall, and that hall leads to an elevator. I usually take the elevator.

The elevator doors opened and I got off on the second floor. Apartment twenty-one is to the left, right next to the elevator. I knocked on the door and then turned the doorknob. I opened the door a crack. The smell of cat piss was immediate.

"Mrs. Phelps?" I called out.

"In here, dear," Mrs. Phelps hollered back, in her shaky, raspy voice. "Make sure the cats don't get out."

I wasn't exactly sure how old Mrs. Phelps was, but it had to be somewhere between one thousand and two thousand years old. She was thin and frail, and had spent the last few years in a wheelchair due to a stroke. Her long hair, a moldy haystack in which a smattering of strands clung stubbornly to golden yellow vibrancy, toppled over the back of her wheelchair. She had a long, horse-like face, so wrinkled it put me in mind of Mrs. Bates' corpse in the finale of *Psycho*. She had none of the facial paralysis often associated with strokes; her speech was likewise unaffected. Her pale blue eyes, though sunken, were merry and alert, and shined with mischief and intelligence. I liked the old bag; she was always good for a laugh and kept me on my toes with her off-the-wall remarks.

I pushed open the door and entered, being careful to watch for one of the six cats that would surely try to escape. Using her feet to propel the wheelchair, she moved slowly down the hall toward me. She was wearing a long red robe. I hoped she was wearing something underneath it. She was wearing the same robe the last three times I repaired something in her apartment. I had hoped she was wearing something underneath the robe those times as well.

"Good morning, Mrs. Phelps. I mean, good afternoon." I shut the door behind me.

"I've told you to call me Maude," she said. She pointed at the small calico kitten in her lap. "Look what I have."

"Oh," I replied, "A new cat. That makes seven, doesn't it?"

"No," she said sadly. "Mr. Pitt passed away last week."

"That's too bad. How is Angelina taking it?"

"She's not eating much, and she stays under my bed most of the day."

I was almost afraid to ask, but I did anyway. "Where is Mr. Pitt now?"

"He's in the freezer."

"In the freezer," I repeated. "How long is he going to stay in the freezer?"

"Until my friend stops by tomorrow. She's taking Mr. Pitt to Eternal Paws to have him cremated."

"Oh."

"I have them all cremated," she explained. "He'll go right up on the shelf with the rest."

I felt a rabbit run over my grave. "The rest?" I asked.

"Haven't I showed you the shelf?"

I was still standing in the hallway with my tools in my hand. "Nope."

"Follow me." She turned and started back down the hall, her feet propelling her as slowly as Fred Flintstone driving through a school zone.

Did I want to see "the shelf?" Of course I did. Was it like a scene from the beginning of many horror films I'd seen? Of course it was, but I wondered why she hadn't shown me the shelf before.

I followed Mrs. Phelps down the long hallway to the living room. When she got to the center of the room, she pointed at a set of three homemade shelves that had been constructed from 1x4 pine boards.

Sitting on the three walnut-stained shelves were about eight or ten small metal boxes. A few of them were old Band-Aid tins and a few were old Altoid containers. Some I didn't recognize.

"There they are," said Mrs. Phelps, waving her arm like a model at a boat show.

Yup, there they are, I thought.

Mrs. Phelps pointed as she listed the contents of each container. "On the top shelf is Muffin. Next to Muffin is Peaches, and next to Peaches is Burt Reynolds and then Matt Damon—"

I wondered why some had conventional cat names and why others were named after celebrities. I wanted to ask, but I also wanted to be home by one.

"—Clarence, Patches, and ... and." She paused and placed her index finger on her chin. "I can't remember who's in the Prince Albert can."

"Is it Prince Albert?" I asked.

Mrs. Phelps chuckled. "Who's buried in Grant's tomb?" she asked. "Oh well, I'll think of it. The last one is Lady Gaga."

I wanted to ask Methuselah's sister how she knew Lady Gaga, but time was a-wastin'. "Thanks for the tour," I said politely. "The faucet?"

"The bathroom. You know where it is."

"Yup." I rubbed my eyes as I walked down the hall. The cat piss was starting to burn. I could hear the sound of running water before I even reached the end of the hall. I pulled open the bathroom door and stepped inside. I searched the wall for a light switch, and then noticed the string hanging from the ceiling light. I pulled the string and the room lit up. Water was pouring from the bathtub spout. I stuck my hand under the stream; it was cold water. I tried to turn the cold faucet, but it wouldn't budge.

I placed my plumbing box on the floor next to the old cast iron, claw-foot tub. I got down on my knees and reached around to the end of the tub, and taking hold of the shut-off, I did my best to turn it. It was as seized up as the faucet.

I opened the lid of my plumbing box and searched for a pipe wrench. I adjusted the pipe wrench to fit over the shut-off handle and tried once again to turn it. It still didn't turn, and I knew if I tried any harder, I would probably break it.

I tossed the wrench back into the box and returned to the living room.

"Mrs. Phelps?" I said.

"Maude," she replied.

"I'm gonna have to run down to the store and grab a few things to fix the faucet. I'll be back up in about twenty minutes."

"Okay, dear," she said, without taking her eyes off the television.

I left Mrs. Phelps' apartment and got back on the elevator. I pressed the number one button, and the doors slid shut.

The best part about working above a hardware store is that almost anything you need is right in the building. The only time I have to run over to Yulee to the Lowe's or Home Depot is if I need lumber or sheetrock.

The elevator doors parted and I stepped off. As I walked down the hallway toward the exit, I pulled out my cell phone and checked the time. I still had an hour and a half to fix the faucet and be home. Things were looking good. I also noticed I had a missed call. I tapped the voice mail icon and listened.

"Rex?" the voice said. "It's Detective Rance. I received a call from a hospital administrator saying someone claiming to be the guy who shot Delbert Haskell called to ask about his condition. If that was you, please don't do that again. Also, they informed me that he's doing just fine. You don't have to call me back."

I hung up the cell and slipped it into my front pocket. "Please don't do that again," I mocked quietly to myself.

Chapter Four

Days of Our Lives was just ending when Gayle walked through the door. "Hey, you're home early," I said.

Gayle was dressed in white jean shorts—the kind cut just above the knee—and a black men's T-shirt with the sleeves rolled up twice. She had her long brown hair pulled back in a ponytail. "We weren't that busy," she said, "and when Toni said someone could leave, I was outta there." She glanced over at the TV screen to see the credits scrolling over the show's iconic hourglass, shook her head. "I can't believe you're still watching this crap."

I put up my hands. "What do you want me to say? It's addicting. Addictive? Which is it?"

Gayle shrugged. "It's neither to me."

"If you ever watched it, you'd be hooked."

"We'll never know."

"Never say never. Hope just found out that Rafe slept with Sammy and—"

"Yeah, I don't care." Gayle kicked off her sneakers and reached back to remove the hair band from her ponytail. I admired her biceps as she pulled the elastic band from her hair and tossed it on the coffee table.

Gayle was in great shape; she went to the gym three or four mornings a week. I had gone to the gym three or four times in my life. My job in construction always kept me in pretty good shape, but I've never had Gayle's enviable muscle tone. Gayle looked like a tough little ass kicker, and I would imagine she kicked her fair share of ass while she was cop in the Navy. She always reminded me of a young Sigourney Weaver, back when she was kicking the shit out of aliens.

Gayle scratched her scalp with her long fingernails as she sat down on the couch beside me. She laid her head on my shoulder and asked, "What's for dinner?"

"I have no idea," I replied.

"I was hoping you were going to make something."

"I had a long day."

"Watching soaps?"

"*One* soap," I said, hoisting my index finger, "*and* I had to change a faucet at the store."

"That's good. At least changing the faucet evens out the watching of women's programming."

"Hey! I shot a guy last night, and I cleaned my gun this afternoon *while* I watched that soap. If that's not the definition of manly, then I don't know what is."

"I guess you got me there." Gayle shifted position and laid her head on my lap. "I need a nap." She closed her eyes.

"Um, am I supposed to just sit here while you nap?"

"Would you?"

"No. I have laundry to fold." I lifted her head and slid out from underneath her. I put her head back down on the couch, and pulled the thin blanket off the back of the couch and draped it over her shoulders. "I'm gonna take a shower and change. I feel like I can still smell cat piss."

"Old Lady Phelps?" Gayle mumbled.

"You know it."

I walked around the couch, stepped over the bloodstain, and went down the hall to the bedroom. After getting undressed, I tossed my dirty cloths into the hamper, something else I never did before retiring.

When I climbed into the shower I slowly breathed in through my nose. *Yep, cat piss*, I thought. I rubbed my fingers on the bar of Irish Spring and jammed them into my nostrils, doing my best to wash away any lingering odor. As I did so, I wondered if it was all in my head.

*****

After my shower I went back down the hall and into the living room; Gayle was snoring away. Not the loud chainsaw type of snoring, but more the quiet, far-off muffled sound of a buffalo in heat. I went to the kitchen in search of something I could throw together for dinner. I checked the fridge and the cupboards.

Gayle and I were the kind of people who shopped for the day, which meant going to Publix several times a week, so there was never an abundance ready food to make at a moment's notice. So unless Gayle wanted breakfast cereal or Ritz crackers for dinner, we were going shopping … or to a restaurant.

I shut the last cupboard door and returned to the living room. There was a little drool in the corner of her mouth, which hung open like one of the Darling Boys on *The Andy Griffith Show*. I wondered if I should wake her. Then, as luck would have it, my cell phone rang and did it for me. She looked up at me annoyed.

"Sorry," I whispered. "Hello?" I answered.

"Is this Rex?" asked a man's voice.

"No," I replied, "but this is."

"What?" he shot back.

"Yes, this is Rex."

"Rex Langley?"

"Yes. May I ask who's calling?"

There was only silence.

I looked at the call screen. The call had ended. The screen read, unavailable.

Gayle cleared her throat. "Who was that?"

"I have no idea." I put the cell back in my front pocket.

"Wrong number?" she asked.

"I don't think so. They asked for me by name."

Gayle sat up and stretched her arms over her head and yawned.

"Good nap?" I asked.

"Short nap," she replied. "Dinner?"

"Grocery store, or restaurant," I answered.

"Restaurant."

"Should we do the back and forth thing, or do you want to just save us some time and aggravation and pick a place?"

"Dairy Queen," she offered.

"Dairy Queen?"

"Yeah. I saw a commercial today at work for the pulled pork sandwich on a pretzel bun and I've been craving one ever since."

"There's a lot of places we could get pulled pork." I wasn't a big fan of fast food, but Gayle was. If it were up to her, we would eat fast food for dinner most nights. Gayle had the lithe body of someone who looked like they watched what they ate. How someone could eat like a truck driver and never gain weight was beyond me. And I wasn't about to tell Gayle she ate like a truck driver. Ever.

"I know, but I really want that pretzel bun thing. That sounds really good," she continued to plead her case. "After we eat we can walk over to Hammerhead's and have a few drinks."

"Okay, if that's what you want." I slipped off my house shoes and walked toward the front door to get my flip-flops. "Let's go."

"I have to shower first."

"Ugh."

"Ugh?"

"I'm hungry."

"It'll only take a minute."

"I'm sure it will," I replied, with no attempt to hide my sarcasm.

Gayle stuck out her tongue, turned, and pranced down the hall, being careful not to step on the bloodstain.

I sat down on the couch and reached for the remote control.

"Babe?" Gayle called out.

"Yeah?" I hollered back.

"You want to have sex before I get in the shower?"

Stupid question. "Yes, please," I shouted. I tossed the remote into the air and ran down the hall as fast as I could.

Chapter Five

We were sitting in a booth at Dairy Queen by 4:30. It usually only takes Gayle a few minutes to shower and get ready to go somewhere informal. Gayle rarely wears makeup; she doesn't need too. She has a natural beauty that's only hindered by layers of paint. I've always felt that most women who wear makeup probably don't need to, but when every magazine and commercial is telling them to hide behind product after product of war paint, it's hard to say no. Gayle never spends much time on her hair either, unless we're going somewhere fancier than Dairy Queen ... like Taco Bell, for example. Dairy Queen only warrants a comb through the hair and a rubber band around a ponytail.

I ordered a bacon cheeseburger and fries with a Coke, and Gayle got just what she had been craving, the pulled pork on a pretzel bun.

"How is it?" I asked. "Is it everything you ever dreamed of?"

Gayle's eyes widened. "Oh!" she replied with a mouthful of pork and pretzel. "This is so good." She dragged out the O in "so" just a little too long. "I should have gotten two of them."

"Yeah, you should have," I said with just a touch of sarcasm. I took another bite of my burger.

Gayle finished chewing and washed it down with a big gulp of root beer. "Mmm-mmm!"

I grinned.

"You have no idea how good this is," Gayle said defensively'

"I believe you."

"You should have ordered one."

"I'm regretting that I didn't. I'll just have to eat through you vicariously." I turned my head and stared out the window, and across the parking lot, at the rear of Hammerhead Beach Bar. I thought about the Bacardi and ginger ale that was awaiting me. Too bad Dairy Queen didn't sell alcohol. A bacon cheeseburger goes much better with a Bacardi and ginger ale than it does with a Coke. I wondered if they had a suggestion box.

I noticed two young men apparently in their late twenties sitting across from us in another booth. One of them was looking in our direction. He quickly averted his eyes when he noticed me watching him.

"Looks like you have a couple admirers," I said.

Gayle looked around the room and her eyes settled on the twenty somethings. The guy looked over again and then away. "Too old for me," she stated.

"I'm forty-eight," I responded.

"Yeah, but you're my husband. I don't mind having an old husband. If I was to get a boyfriend however, he would have to be around twenty-one or twenty-two. Those two are obviously in their late twenties—or maybe early thirties."

"Old husband?" I asked.

"That's the only part of that that bothered you?"

"I don't think I heard anything after that."

"I meant old-*er*."

"Oh," I said, nodding my head, "old-*er*. That's much better than just plain old."

Gayle went back to her sandwich. I went back to my burger. And the young men went back to sneaking peeks at Gayle. I couldn't help sneaking peeks at Gayle either, so I knew just how they felt. Gayle didn't have the largest breasts in the world, but her small Bs looked pretty damn good, and were very noticeable, in the tank top and Victoria's Secret push-up bra she was wearing. I wonder how the "gentlemen" would react when she got up from the booth and they saw the shorts she was wearing.

Gayle looked over once again and caught one of them staring. "What!" she said … a little louder than I was comfortable with. "What are you looking at?" She was using her scary military voice. It was one of the things the government let her keep when she retired. "You never saw a pair of tits before?"

"Oh, Christ," I whispered.

Neither boy said a word. They looked a little frightened.

"I didn't think so," said Gayle. "Now eat your burgers before I come over there and shove 'em up your asses."

The boys did as they were told, only they were eating a little faster than before. They probably had somewhere to be.

"I think the one kid was eating a pulled pork sandwich," I offered.

Gayle nodded her head. "I knew that kid had good taste the minute I saw him staring at my rack."

I just shook my head.

By the time we finished our dinner, Gayle's admirers had left. They never gave her another look. I'm guessing they took her threat seriously. We emptied our trays and walked across the parking lot to Hammerheads.

As we walked along holding hands I asked, "Should I give Paul and Lori a call and tell them to meet us for a drink?"

"Good idea," said Gayle.

I pulled out my cell and dialed Paul's number.

Paul and Lori Farber had been friends of ours almost since the day they moved to Amelia Island.

Lori owned and ran the bookstore in town: Island Books. Paul had been a real estate attorney with a large firm in Manhattan but decided to trade the hustle and bustle of the big city for the quiet, laid-back vibe of island life. After the two moved here with their three children, Paul opened a small office on North Third Street.

"They'll be here in about an hour," I said.

"Awesome," Gayle replied.

We made our way along the concrete sidewalk between the bar and the two story wooden deck.

"Grab that table," I said, pointing to the empty four top next to the railing. "I'll get our drinks."

I took a right into the building' Gayle hung a left and went up the ramp to the deck. I took off my sunglasses and folded them over the front of my shirt.

The interior of Hammerhead's is dark and shadowy. You wouldn't even know you were in a beach bar if it weren't for the words beach and bar being in the name. The interior is reminiscent of a smoky old roadside pool hall, like the kind I imagine thrived along Route 66 in its heyday. There are, in fact, several pool tables in the joint; occasionally one hears the sharp, castanet-like snick of cue meeting ball rising above the merrymaking of the boisterous crowd. The floor is wooden planks, the walls are horizontal wainscoting, and the low ceiling is beaded pine boards with exposed beams, every bit of it stained dark walnut.

Like most Friday nights, Sandi was behind the bar. Sandi was blonde and petite, with large fake boobs. She was wearing Daisy Dukes and a bikini top that must have been her little sister's. There were stars over one breast and red and white stripes over the other. *God bless America*. Sandi's abs told the story of a young woman who performed at least one hundred million sit-ups per day.

"Hey, Mr. Langley!" said Sandi, flashing a big smile.

"Hey, Sandi," I returned.

"What can I get for ya?"

"A Bacardi and ginger ale and a Margarita."

"Comin' right up."

Sandi turned around to make the drinks. I turned around as well, because I didn't want to get caught staring at anything I wasn't supposed to be staring at.

"Hey, Rex," I heard a voice call out.

I turned to see Larry, the owner of Hammerheads, standing near the men's room. I nodded. "Hey, Larry."

"I heard you shot Delbert Haskell last night."

Sandi's head whipped around.

"Yeah," I replied. "He a friend of yours?"

"You shot somebody?" Sandi asked. She gaped at me in wide-eyed wonder. Larry came up beside her and, with one hand atop her head and the other under her chin, closed the orifice before a fly got in. Sandi elbowed him in the ribs, hard.

"He's no friend of mine," said Larry. "He comes in here now and then. Had to throw him out a few times."

"Troublemaker, huh?" I inquired.

"You could say that. You better watch yourself," Larry warned. "I don't imagine his brothers are too happy about it."

"Brothers?" I asked. My voice cracked a little when I said it. "How many brothers does he have?"

"Two," Sandi offered. She had completely halted the drink making operation. "They're mean."

Two mean brothers, I thought. "Hey," I said, "he broke into *my* house. Besides, I only shot him in the leg. He'll be fine."

"You better hope he'll be fine," said Larry.

"Yeah," Sandi agreed, slowly nodding her wide-eyed head. "You better hope he'll be fine."

"Thanks, Sandi," I said. "I got it the first time."

Sandi shrugged and turned back around to make Gayle's margarita. When she was finished she placed both drinks on the bar and slid them forward. "There ya go. One Bacardi and ginger, and one marg on the rocks."

"Marg," I grumbled under my breath. I tossed a twenty onto the bar and Sandi made change. I left her a three-dollar tip and exited the bar.

There wasn't a cloud in the sky and the sun was bright. I wanted to put my sunglasses back on, but I had a drink in each hand. I closed one eye and squinted with the other. Gayle was the only one on the deck; it was early yet. The crowd wouldn't pick up for another hour or two. Spring break had ended and summer vacation hadn't started, so it wouldn't be too crowded.

I walked up the ramp and onto the deck. Gayle was seated under a bright yellow Corona Light umbrella at one of the four wooden tables that sat out in the sun. Four other tables occupied the shaded area underneath the upper deck. I set Gayle's drink in front of her. "Here's your *marg*," I said.

"Thanks."

I placed my drink on the table and put my sunglasses back on. "There, that's better." I took a seat adjacent to Gayle.

"Who's working tonight?" Gayle asked.

"Sandi."

"She called it a marg?"

"Yup."

"College girls, huh?"

"They're re-dic," I said.

"Def," Gayle agreed.

We sipped our drinks and stared out across the street and over the water. A DJ was setting up his equipment on the deck's second level.

"Oh," I said."

"That's quite enough of the brainless college girl speak," said Gayle.

"By the way," I said, changing back to normal human being speak. "Delbert Haskell has two mean brothers."

"I know."

"You knew?"

"Of course I knew. Beau and Bobby Joe. Both meaner than snakes."

"How did you know that?"

"It's a small town, Rex."

"Yeah, I guess," I agreed. "Why didn't you say something?"

"About his brothers?"

"Yeah."

"I didn't want to worry you."

"*You* didn't want to worry *me?*" I shot back.

"Well, you know how you get."

"No. How do I get?"

Gayle took a big sip of her margarita. I knew she was stalling for time, trying to figure out the best way to word what she was about to say. "You know, all freaked out like you get."

"All freaked out," I repeated.

"Yeah. I didn't want you to start worrying that his brothers were going to exact their revenge on you." Gayle made finger quotes around *exact their revenge*.

I stared at Gayle for a second. Sometimes it's hard to be married to a woman who was a military cop for twenty years. Sometimes a lesser man might feel like less of a man. "Using finger quotes when you say 'exact their revenge' doesn't make it sound foolish, ya know. Sometimes people do exact revenge."

Gayle slowly shook her head. "I knew it."

"Drink your marg," I said.

Chapter Six

Saturday morning I had a headache, probably from the Bacardi and gingers. Gayle was up and making breakfast. Of course, she didn't have a headache. Not only could Gayle eat like a truck driver, she could also drink like a sailor; I imagine it was because she used to be one. Yeah, that's my wife. Someday I hope to teach her to walk and to talk and to dress like a regular lady, I does.

"Scrambled or over easy?" Gayle asked when she heard me walk in behind her.

"Scrambled," I said. I could see she also had some bacon in another pan and toast sitting in the toaster ready to go down. I grabbed a coffee cup out of the cupboard and poured myself a cup. "You bring in the paper?" I asked.

"Nope."

I carried my coffee to the front door. I opened it and squatted down to pick up the paper. As I rose I noticed the black Jeep Cherokee parked across the street, at the entrance to the cul-de-sac, facing in the wrong direction. The windows were slightly tinted, but I could see the outline of its occupant. It looked as though he was staring in my direction. I stared back for a few second, squinting my eyes to get a better look. There was no movement inside the vehicle. I swung the door closed.

When I returned to the kitchen I said, matter-of-factly, "There's a Jeep parked out front."

"Yeah?"

"Yeah, and it's facing the wrong way."

"And?"

"There's a guy in the driver's seat."

Gayle said nothing.

"It looked like he was staring at the house," I added.

Gayle slowly turned around. I knew she was smirking *before* she even turned around. "What are you getting at?" she asked. "Don't tell me a strange car's going to turn you into a raving paranoiac."

"Never mind," I said, and went back into the living room to read my paper. As I sat down on the couch, I gazed out the front window; the Jeep was gone.

LOCAL MAN SHOT DURING HOME INVASION, the headline read. *Son of a bitch.* I read the entire story.

My name was left out. I was glad, but by now everyone in town already knew it was me, including Delbert's brothers.

As I read through the paper my eyes kept going back and forth from the news to the front window. Maybe Gayle was right. Maybe I was being paranoid.

Halfway through a story about an old guy who was carjacked out on the Amelia Island Parkway, my cell phone rang. The ring startled me and I flinched. *Yup, paranoid*, I thought.

"Hello?" I said.

"Rex? It's Kevin."

"Hey, Kevin. What's up?"

"Got a little problem over here at the store."

"When don't you?" I caught sight of Gayle out of the corner of my eye. She was holding two plates.

"Breakfast," Gayle mouthed silently. She walked over and set the plates on the coffee table, and took a seat at the other end of the couch.

"What's the problem?" I asked.

"That drainpipe in apartment twenty-four is dripping down into the store again—well, running more than dripping now. You think you could take a look at it?"

"Sure." I looked at the time on my cell. "I'll be there at noon."

"Sounds good. I put a bucket under it for now."

"Okay. I'll see you in a couple hours."

"What's up?" Gayle asked, when I hung up the cell.

"Leaky pipe at the store."

"Boy, for a guy who doesn't work Mondays, Fridays, or weekends, you sure work a lot of Mondays, Fridays, and weekends."

I picked up my breakfast plate and placed it on my lap. "Yeah, I know," I replied with a hint of irritation.

"Maybe I'll ride over with you," Gayle suggested. "I wanted to stop by the bookstore any way."

"Sounds good to me," I replied, with a mouthful of scrambled eggs.

I had finished my breakfast, gotten myself another cup of coffee, and returned to my newspaper when my cell phone rang again.

"Hello?"

"*Rex*?" a voice asked.

I could tell by the way he said my name who it was. "Detective Rance," I said. "How's it going?"

"Super," he replied.

"To what do I owe the pleasure?"

"Two things," Rance began. "One, Delbert Haskell's brother, Bobby Joe, called me this morning. He wants charges brought against you for shooting his little brother."

"Can he do that?" I asked.

"He can want all he wants, but the DA won't bring charges against you."

"Well, that's a good thing … isn't it?"

"Maybe."

"Maybe?"

"I just want you to steer clear of those two boys, Rex."

"Isn't there something *you* can do?"

"Like what?"

"I don't know … arrest him."

"For what? He hasn't broken any laws. He hasn't even made any threats," Rance said condescendingly. "I just want you to be aware of what's going on."

I sighed. "Okay. Thanks, Rance."

"It's the least I could do."

"I guess so," I agreed. "What's the second thing?"

"Second thing?"

"You said there were two things you wanted to tell me," I reminded him.

"Oh yeah, I called the hospital this morning to see how Delbert was doing."

"And?"

"He's got a pretty bad infection. They had to open him up again."

"That's just great," I groaned. "He's not going to die is he?"

Rance chuckled. "You better hope not. I don't think his brother's would be too pleased with that."

"Keep me posted," I said, and hung up.

"What now?" Gayle asked.

"Looks like the Haskell's might be looking to exact some of that revenge we were talking about." This time I made the finger quotes.

Gayle rolled her eyes. "Here we go."

Chapter Seven

I dropped Gayle off at the bookstore and got to the Collin's Hardware a little after noon. I went into the store first to see how much damage there was to the ceiling. Christine was behind the counter waiting on a customer.

"Kevin around?" I asked.

"I think he's down in his office," Christine replied.

"Thanks," I said, and kept walking. I made a right at the end of the checkout counter and a left down the aisle with brooms, shovels, sledge hammers, rakes, and hoes. At the end of the aisle was a doorway with no door. When I was halfway down the aisle, Mark Collins, Kevin's son, exited the doorway.

Mark was about five-seven and rail thin, with a reddish beard. I had never seen him without a ball cap. I wondered if he was bald like his dad, or if he just liked wearing ball caps.

"Hey, Mark," I said. "Your dad down there?"

"Yeah, he's at his desk."

"Thanks." I walked through the opening, made a quick left, and went down the stairs to the basement.

Kevin sat at his desk pecking at his keyboard as he glared at the screen over his reading glasses.

"Porn?" I joked.

"No," he replied. "Just paying bills." He stopped what he was doing and rolled his desk chair back a few feet. "You see the ceiling?"

"Nope."

"You go up to twenty-four yet?"

"Nope. I was going to see if you wanted to run up there with me."

Kevin turned up his nose. "I don't *want* to."

I grinned. "The place still pretty bad?"

Kevin nodded his head. "I don't know what's wrong with that guy. He just won't clean the place up. I've warned him several times and even threatened him with eviction."

"So, I gotta go up by myself?"

Kevin groaned. "No," he said defeatedly. "I'll go up with you." He pulled himself up out of his chair with a groan. Kevin was about the same height as his son, but with an extra fifty pounds or so.

I turned and went back up the stairs, and Kevin followed.

"Do you have a key for twenty-four?" Kevin asked.

"Not with me," I replied.

We stopped at the front counter and Kevin pulled a key from a large metal box full of keys. The key was attached to a small plastic tag with the number twenty-four on it.

"This might be it," Kevin said. "Who knows? I've changed these doorknobs so many times over the years."

Kevin's father had purchased the building that housed Collins' Hardware over forty years ago. After he bought the building, he moved the hardware store from its previous location, down the street, to its current location.

Kevin and I walked out the front door and around the side of the building. We made our way down the sidewalk, through the door, and down the long hallway to the elevator. When the doors parted we stepped onto the elevator and Kevin pressed the number two button.

When the doors parted again, we stepped off onto the second floor. Maude Phelps was parked in her wheelchair, half in, and half out of her apartment. She smiled when she saw us.

"Tiny Tim," said Maude, apropos of nothing.

Kevin and I looked at each other, and then back at Maude.

"Excuse me?" I said.

She walked two fingers across the palm of her hand. "You know—'Tiptoe Through the Tulips'. Tiny Tim."

I cocked my head. "I know who Tiny Tim is," I told her. "What about him?"

"It was Tiny Tim in the Prince Albert can."

It took me a second. "Oh. Gotcha. Tiny Tim."

Kevin didn't look any less puzzled after she said it was her cat. He turned and started toward apartment twenty-four. I followed.

"Have a nice day, Mrs. Phelps," I said.

"It's Maude," she called back.

I gave her a wave over my shoulder.

Kevin knocked on twenty-four. "What the heck was that all about?" he asked.

"She was showing me her dead cats yesterday and—"

The door opened with a creak. "Yeah?"

"Edgar, I have to come in and look at that drainpipe," Kevin said. "It's leaking into the store again."

"You posta gimme a twenty-four are notice iffin ya wanna come in," Edgar replied.

"Just open the door, Edgar," said Kevin. "I ain't got time for your crap."

Edgar grinned. He only had about four teeth and three of them were black. "I giss I ken let ya break dem rules dis once." He stepped back and pulled open the door. The stench was overwhelming. I tried not to let it show on my face.

Edgar was in his late forties. He was short and wiry. His ears, nose, and lips were far too big for his head, and he had long skinny arms, and long skinny fingers. He was pale, due to almost never leaving his apartment. If you Googled homunculus, a picture of Edgar would surly pop up. It was obvious to anyone who came in contact with him, that he was just not normal; mentally, or physically. When Edgar spoke, he had an accent all his own. I had heard a lot of different southern accents in my life, but whatever the hell that was that Edgar spoke, I'll never know.

We walked in past him and down the hall to his kitchen. I glanced inside each room as we passed. Every room was full of hoarder treasure with pathways leading this way and that. When we arrived at the kitchen, it was just as bad. A path led from the doorway to the sink. The rest of the room was filled from floor to ceiling with discarded milk jugs, newspaper, garbage, bags, and boxes, and whatever else Edgar couldn't part with. Sitting on the floor in front of the cracked pipe were five cases of Hidden Valley ranch dressing, each containing twenty-four bottles, so the label said. I bent down and slid the boxes out of the way.

"What did you need with a hundred and twenty bottles of ranch dressing, Edgar?" I asked. Not really wanting to know the answer.

"Thay's own sale at da Publix," Edgar replied. "Ya never know when ya gonna needum."

"Better to have too many than not enough, I guess," I deadpanned. I could see Kevin shake his head out of the corner of my eye. I moved a few more things out of the way. "There it is."

Kevin craned his neck for a better look over my shoulder. "You think you can patch it?" he asked.

I tried to rub away some of the old flaky paint and rust from the pipe and my thumb went right through it. "Nope," I responded. "Don't think it can be patched. I'm going to have to pull it out of here and replace it with PVC."

"When do you think you can do it?" Kevin asked.

"You ain't gonna mess up da place, is ya?" asked Edgar. His eyes bugged out in alarm.

"I'll try my best not to," I assured him.

"Thanky," Edgar said.

I looked back over my shoulder at Kevin. "Let's talk out in the hall," I whispered.

Kevin nodded. He backed up, turned, and started for the door. I followed him down the hall.

Edgar said, "I'll sees yous boys later," and shut the door behind us.

Kevin and I walked toward the elevator. "I can't work in there like that," I said. "It's bad enough being in there for a few minutes."

"What should we do?" Kevin asked.

I shrugged. "You have to get him out of there so we can clean that place up."

"I've threatened him with eviction so many times trying to get him to clean the place up. He always says he'll clean it up, but he never does."

"I don't know. Hoarding's an addiction, same as alcohol or drugs; can't just be cured overnight." I pontificated. "How long has he been here?"

"Him and his brother, Everette, moved in there about ten years ago, maybe. His brother moved out three years ago. I feel bad for the guy. He has no one."

"I know, but if someone from code enforcement ever sees that place—"

Kevin put up his hand. "I know. I know."

"Is there an empty apartment we can put him in until we get this one cleaned up? We can move him back in after I'm done."

Kevin thought for a second. "The only thing empty is the store room on the second floor."

"It was an apartment at one time," I offered. "It has a bathroom and kitchen."

Kevin breathed in deep and loudly sighed. "I guess," he said. He looked at the floor, slowly shaking his head. "Sounds like it's going to be a lot of work."

"It's either that or throw him out into the street."

"I couldn't live with myself."

"I know."

"Can you get the pipe to stop leaking until he's out?"

"I'll try to wrap something around it temporarily. No guarantee on how long it'll hold though."

"Sounds good." Kevin sighed again.

"Stop sighing," I scolded.

We walked back toward the elevator. Maude Phelps was still sitting in her doorway.

"Tiny Tim," she said, on our way by. "The cat in the Price Albert can. His name was Tiny Tim."

"Yup, you already told me," I said. I stopped. "Why did you name your cat Tiny Tim?"

Kevin didn't stop. I guess he wasn't interested in why Maude would name her cat after the ukulele-strumming balladeer. I, on the other hand, wouldn't be able to sleep not knowing.

"That damn song," said Maude. "Couldn't get that damn song out of my head."

"'Tiptoe Though the Tulips'?"

"Yes." She pointed down the hall in the direction I had just come from. "Edgar's idiot brother Everette walked around singing that damn song all the time. If he wasn't singing it, he was whistling it. 'Tiptoe

Through the Tulips' echoing through the halls at all hours of the day and night."

"If you hated it so much, then why did you name your cat Tiny Tim?"

"You listen to that day and night and see if that's not the first thing that pops into *your* head when you get up in the mornin'."

I chuckled. "I guess you're probably right." I turned to see Kevin holding the elevator door open for me. He had an impatient look in his eye as he glared my way.

"I was glad when that idiot moved out," Maude commented.

"You have a nice day, Mrs. Phelps."

"Maude," she said.

I stepped onto the elevator and the door closed behind me.

"So, what about the dead cats?" Kevin asked.

"Maude has her cats who have passed away on a shelf in her living room."

"Good God!" said Kevin.

"It's their ashes," I assured him.

"Oh. That's better."

"There is a whole dead cat in her freezer, however."

"Swell."

"His name is Brad Pitt."

"Oh, yeah? And I suppose the cat's mate was Angelina Jolie."

"Naturally. Poor thing's taking it pretty hard. She's in mourning."

"Wow," said Kevin, "you really need to get a life."

Chapter Eight

Monday morning after Gayle left for work, I decided to drive over to the hardware store to see how Kevin was coming along with getting Edgar out of his apartment. I pulled up to the curb in front of the store and parked.

Mark was behind the checkout counter. "Hey," I said.

Mark looked up from some paperwork he had in front of him and nodded. "What's up?" he asked.

"Your dad around?" I asked. I never knew if I was supposed to refer to Kevin as *dad* when I was speaking to Mark, or if he would rather me call him Kevin. I guess calling him by his name would sound a little more professional, but it also seemed odd to me to do that. Besides, Mark didn't seem to care either way. I made myself a mental note to someday ask his preference.

Mark glanced up at the old schoolhouse-style clock over the entrance door. "He went to breakfast. He should be back any second."

"Did he break the news to Edgar?"

"What news?"

That's a bad sign, I thought. Kevin loved to put things off. "About moving out of his apartment."

Mark shook his head. He looked a little confused. "I didn't hear anything about it."

"I wonder if Edgar heard anything about it."

"I have no idea." Mark returned his attention to the papers and receipts on the counter.

"Hey, Mark," I said.

He looked up again. "Yeah?"

"You guys carry those little plastic alarms that go on windows? The ones that come in two pieces; one part goes on the sash," I described, "and the other on the frame. When someone opens the window, the alarm goes off."

"I know what you're talking about. They're plastic, and battery-operated." He held his thumb and index finger about three inches apart. "About yay big?"

"That's the ones."

"We don't have them in stock, but I can probably get them from the warehouse."

"How long's it take to get them?"

"They should be here Wednesday morning."

"That would be great. Can you order me some?"

"Sure." Mark grabbed a pen and notepad. "How many you want?"

I thought for a second, mentally counting the windows in my house. "Thirteen," I said.

"Lucky number thirteen," Mark commented while jotting down my request. "I'll order them when I get done with what I'm doing."

"Great," I said. "Thanks." I headed for the exit. "Tell Kevin I'll stop back by later." *Yeah*, I thought, *that didn't sound natural. I'll stick with dad.*

I exited the building and made a hard right. I walked a few steps to Amelia Island Coffee and went inside.

Amelia Island Coffee was a quaint little coffee shop. With its exposed brick walls and checkout counter wrapped in reclaimed wooden planks, it looked like the perfect setting for a Hallmark Channel love story.

Janice Godfrey, all five foot nothing of her, stood behind the counter. She wore a white apron and her black hair was up in a tight little bun. Janice was in her early sixties, took good care of herself, and had a pretty good build. I guess I'm too old to be considered a "cougar hunter," but I see nothing wrong with appreciating older women. Like Gayle says: you can look all you want, but don't touch.

"Mornin', Rex," said Janice.

"Morning, Janice," I returned. "Can I get a medium coffee ... black?"

"Comin' right up." While Janice prepared my order she hummed no particular tune. When she finished she set the cup on the counter. "Heard you had a little trouble out to your place the other night." She said it loud, and I looked around the room. The few other patrons sitting at tables were now interested at the trouble that I had out at my place the other night.

"Sure," I replied. I took hold of my cup. It was almost too hot to touch.

"Shot young Delbert Haskell," she remarked.

"Yeah, I know. I was there."

"His brothers ain't gonna be too happy about that," came a voice from behind me. I turned to see who it was. It was Lloyd Cushing. He was grinning and nodding his head. My eyes focused on his off-colored front tooth, the one that seemed to be longer and wider than the one right next to it.

"Yeah, I know, Lloyd," I replied.

"They's ornery boys," Lloyd added.

"Thanks, Lloyd," I said. I tossed a five-dollar bill on the counter, and Janice made change. "Keep it."

"Thanks, Rex," said Janice. She dropped the change into a glass tip jar on the counter. "You take care of yourself, Rex."

"I will, Janice." I turned and walked outside. When I got out there, I decided to take a seat at one of the two wrought iron tables located out front. I turned the chair so I was facing Centre Street, and crossed my legs. I removed the lid from my cup and blew into it. I took a small sip. It was far too hot to take a big gulp.

I sat there for about twenty minutes while nursing my coffee. I watched cars go by. I watched people go by. Many of the people I knew, but most of them I didn't. The tourists are always easy to spot. Like tourists anywhere, they walk around pointing at things. On Centre Street in Fernandina Beach they point at the old brick buildings. They point at the clock tower high above the court house. They point at the old train depot. They sit on the bench next to the statue of David Yulee, the founder of the Florida Railroad Company, and have someone take their picture. Most of them have never heard of David Yulee, but hey, it's a statue on a bench, so what the hell. Mostly tourists stand out in the middle of Centre Street and take selfies with the old Palace Saloon Coca-Cola sign in the background.

Just as I finished my coffee and got up from the table, I saw Kevin Collins strolling down the street. I walked back over to the entrance door of the hardware store and waited for him to get there.

"Rex," he said.

"Kevin," I replied.

"What's up?" he asked.

"Did you talk to Edgar?" I asked.

"Not yet."

"Ugh."

"I didn't know what to tell him."

"I thought we were going to move him into the store room for a week or so."

"Do you think that's legal?"

"I don't think the way he's living now is legal."

"I guess you're right."

"So you're going to talk to him then?"

Kevin sighed. "I guess."

I smiled. "Do you want me to talk to him?"

"Would ya?"

"Sure. I'll go up now."

"Thanks. I owe ya."

"Yeah you do," I agreed. "You want to come up with me?"

"Nope." Kevin turned and went inside the store.

I walked around and down the alleyway to the doors that lead to the elevator. When I got off the elevator on the second floor I half-expected Maude Phelps to be sitting in her doorway; she wasn't. I made my way down the hall to apartment twenty-four and knocked. I waited a few seconds and knocked again. I tried the doorknob; it was unlocked. I pushed open the door a foot and stuck my head into the stench.

"Edgar?" I called out. No answer. I tried to close my nostrils as I stood there waiting. "Edgar!" I hollered. I pushed the door open the rest of the way and went in. I walked down the hall and stopped at the first bedroom. I wasn't sure if that was Edgar's room or not, but I peeked in cautiously, not wanting to see exactly what he did when he was alone in his bedroom. He wasn't in there, so I went on to the next door; it was the bathroom. It stunk pretty bad. With the amount of … stuff, for lack of a better word, that Edgar had stacked in his bathtub, it was obvious he hadn't bathed or showered in quite some time.

"Edgar?" I said one more time.

I peered into the second bedroom and then the kitchen. There was Edgar lying on the kitchen floor. Every hair on my arms stood on end. It startled me, and I backed up a step. I felt a wave of fear come over me. I wasn't sure why; there was nothing in Edgar's apartment that was going to harm me. Other than seeing someone in a casket at a funeral home viewing, however, I had never seen a dead body in my life. I sure as hell never walked in on one unexpectedly.

I stood in the doorway staring down at Edgar, my heart pounding. An old wooden chair, a yellow spindle back, lay tipped over. One leg was broken. The chair was on its side between Edgar and me. Edgar was lying in the pathway that ran from where I was standing, to the sink. He was on his right side; the way his neck was twisted, I knew it was broken. I was a bit surprised that Edgar's broken neck looked a lot like broken necks I'd seen in movies. There was blood on the edge of the countertop and a smear of it down the front of the sink base. I felt a little nauseous, but I had felt a little nauseous before I saw Edgar lying there. I pulled out my cell phone and dialed 911.

I spoke with a friendly young woman and told her who I was, where I was, and what had happened. She wanted me to check for a pulse. I told her there was no need. She wanted me to check any way. I told her I didn't want too. She told me to stay where I was, and that someone would be there shortly. She wanted me to stay on the line with her, but I hung up, and called down stairs to see if Kevin was still in the building.

"Hey," I said.

"What?" Kevin replied.

"We have a little problem."

"What's that?"

"Edgar is dead."

There was a long pause.

"Did you hear what I said?" I asked.

"Edgar, upstairs?" Kevin asked.

"Do you know another Edgar?" I asked.

At that point I could hear a siren. The sound came from the open front window down the hall. I could also hear it in the phone.

"Are you still up there?" Kevin asked.

"Yup."

"I'll be right up."

I hung up the cell and stepped out into the hallway. The elevator doors parted a minute later and two paramedics wheeled a gurney into the hall.

"Right in there," I said, pointing into Edgar's apartment. "But you aren't getting that stretcher in there."

"Why not?" one of them asked.

"He was a hoarder," I replied.

"Swell," the other one said.

They left the gurney where it was and went inside.

"All the way to the end ... in the kitchen," I told them.

I watched from the doorway as they made their way down the narrow, garbage-lined path.

The elevator opened again; it was Kevin this time. "Where is he?" he asked.

"Kitchen floor," I said. "The paramedics are in there now.

The elevator opened again a few minutes later, and off stepped Detective Calvin Rance. He took one look at me and said, "Figures."

I shrugged.

"Where there's trouble, there's you," Rance said.

"I don't know what you want me to say," I replied.

"Yeah, me either," he said. He nodded to Kevin on his way past him and into Edgar's apartment.

"All the way to the end," I said. "In the kitchen."

"Thanks," Rance responded, "you're a big help."

"I don't think he means that," Kevin said.

"He loves me," I deadpanned.

Kevin and I stood there for a minute or two with our arms crossed, discussing the weather.

"Supposed to rain tomorrow," I said.

"That's what they're saying," Kevin replied.

"Rex!" Rance shouted.

"Yeah!" I hollered back.

"Get in here!"

I turned to Kevin. "You think I should ask him to say please?"

"I think you better get in there."

I walked into the apartment and down the hall. Halfway to the kitchen, one of the paramedics and I had to pass each other. It wasn't easy; the path down the hall was only a one-man path. We squeezed past each other and continued on our respective ways.

I poked my head into the kitchen. "Yeah?"

"This just how you found him?" Rance asked.

"Yup."

"You didn't touch anything?"

"Nope."

Rance looked around the kitchen and through an opening into the dining room. He stood on his tiptoes and craned his neck to see through the dining room and into the living room.

"What are you looking for?" I asked.

"How the hell would I know?" Rance replied. "I can't believe someone could live like this."

The paramedic returned from outside the apartment; he was carrying a black body bag, folded up.

"Let me get out of your way," I said. We squeezed by each other again. "We have to stop meeting like this," I told the young man. He looked at me like I was stupid. I didn't mind. People had looked at me like that plenty of times in my life.

"Don't go too far," Rance said.

"Yup," I replied.

When I got back to Kevin, he asked, "What did he want?"

"He wanted to know if I thought you killed Edgar," I said.

Kevin's eyes widened. "What?" he gasped. "Why would *I* kill him?"

"I don't know, Kevin. Why does anybody kill anyone?"

"What did you tell him?"

"I told him you wanted the poor guy out of this apartment pretty badly."

"Jesus Christ! Why did you tell him that?" Beads of sweat were already forming on Kevin's forehead and upper lip. He wiped his brow and smeared the sweat on his pants.

I put my hand on his shoulder. "I'm busting your balls, pal. He just wanted to know if I touched anything."

Kevin took a deep breath and let it out. His head dropped. "You're a real asshole."

"Funny though, right?"

"Not at all."

Chapter Nine

After Detective Rance had asked me a few more questions, I left the hardware store and went in search of Gayle. I walked across the street toward the bookstore to see if she was there. I knew she and Lori were probably still at lunch, but with as many as thirty diners, cafes, and bistros in a five-block radius, I was not about to go hunting for them. If Gayle had her way, they would be at Burger King. Lori would have tried to talk her into something nicer, like David's—but I knew they didn't open until five—or Lulu's. Gayle was a meat and potatoes kind of gal who didn't go for hoity-toity atmosphere and prices to match. They would probably settle on The Crab Trap or The Salty Pelican, two popular joints that didn't put on any airs.

I stepped onto the brick walkway between the curb and the sidewalk. I tried to see in through the front windows, but the shade of the big old mossy oak out front just wasn't enough to cut down on the glare on such a bright and sunny day.

The bookstore's entrance door was propped open and I went inside. I like books as well as the next guy, but the woodblock prints that decorated the walls—depicting literary luminaries ranging from Shakespeare to Edgar Allan Poe—were intimidating. Then there were the books here, the books there, books everywhere. I always felt a little ignorant when I was in Lori's shop, realizing how many "must read" books I'd never read, and probably never would.

Kathrine, one of Lori Farber's employees, was removing new books from a shipping box and placing them on a shelf.

"Hey, Kathrine," I said.

Kathrine turned slightly and looked over her shoulder. "Good afternoon, Mr. Langley," she said. "How are you today?"

"Good," I told her. "Gayle and Lori around?"

"They're still at lunch."

"Do you know where they went?"

"The Crab Trap, I'm pretty sure."

"Thanks." I turned and headed back across the street. *Huh,* I thought, *The Crab Trap, one of the two places I was thinking.* My mind wandered as I walked down Second Street. I wondered what else I could guess right. *Where would they be sitting?* I wondered. *Probably at the bar. Gayle would be facing the door; she would order a beer and a burger. Lori would order a sandwich; something healthy, and a fruity drink.*

I reached the entrance of The Crab Trap. The two-story stucco building sat at the corner of Second Street and Alachua Street. It was concrete with red trim. The Crab Trap's sign was a big wooden crab that hung on a pole over the door. I pulled open the door and went inside.

When my eyes adjusted to the darkness, I scanned the dining room. *Holy crap*, I was right, they were sitting at the bar. Gayle was sitting facing the entrance door with a burger and a beer in front of her. *Four for four*, I thought. They didn't see me until I was right next to them.

"Hey," Gayle said surprised. "What are you doing here?"

"I needed a drink," I said. I noticed Lori's beer, and the garden salad in front of her. *One for two*, I thought. *Not bad.*

Gayle studied my face after I told her I needed a drink. "What's the matter?" she asked.

The bartender walked up. "What can I get for ya, sir?" he asked.

I glanced over at Gayle's beer. "Whatever she's having," I said.

"Comin' right up." He turned and went to the tap handles.

I turned back to Gayle. "Remember that guy I told you about?"

"What guy?" Gayle asked.

"The hoarder above Collins'."

"Yeah, what about him?"

"He's dead."

Lori did a spit take worthy of Mel Brooks.

Gayle's reaction was much calmer. "What happened?" she asked.

"I knocked on his door and when he didn't answer, I went inside. He was lying on his kitchen floor … dead."

"Heart attack?" Lori asked.

"Broken neck," I replied.

Lori put her hand to her mouth. "Oh, my."

"Yeah," I said.

"How did it happen?" Gayle asked.

"The detective said he thinks he fell off a chair while standing on it."

"What was he doing up on a chair?" Lori asked.

"How would I know?" I replied.

"I guess that solves your problem," said Gayle.

"What problem?" Lori asked.

"Rex and Kevin were trying to get the guy out of the place so they could do some repairs," Gayle explained. "Maybe they'll bury the old bugger with all his trash … at the city dump."

Lori knew Gayle pretty well, but everybody in our circle of friends was often surprised at her brashness and dark humor. "That's terrible, Gayle," she said.

"It was a joke," Gayle defended.

"Not funny," said Lori.

Gayle took a bite of her burger and washed it down with a big gulp of draft beer.

"Here ya go, sir," said the bartender, sliding my pint glass in front of me.

"Put it on her tab," I said, throwing a thumb in Gayle's direction. I downed half the beer in my first gulp and let out a sigh. "I needed that."

"I bet," Lori said.

"Dead bodies upset you, sweetheart?" Gayle joked.

"Yup," I replied, and took another swig. "Don't like dead bodies at all."

"I just hope Edgar's ghost doesn't come back and exact his revenge on you from the grave," Gayle said. "After all, the last thing on his mind before he died was you kicking him out of his apartment."

I glared at Gayle. "Thanks, Gayle. That's really helpful."

Lori and Gayle both chuckled at that.

Chapter Ten

Tuesday morning Gayle and I both left for work at the same time. No sooner did I walk through the front door of Collins' Hardware than my cell phone rang.

"Hello?" I said.

"Rex?"

"Yeah?"

"It's Detective Rance."

"Hey, pal. What's up?"

"Pal?" he questioned.

I didn't respond.

"Delbert Haskell died last night."

"What?"

"Delbert Haskell … he died last night," Rance repeated.

"Uh," was all I could say.

Rance waited a few seconds and then asked, "Did you hear me, Rex?"

"Um … yeah, I heard you. How?"

"The infection in his leg," Rance replied. "The doctor said his body just couldn't fight it off."

I looked around the store. Christine stood behind the checkout counter. Mark and Kevin were standing to my right; all eyes were on me. "So … so, what now?"

"Nothing," Rance said. "I spoke with the district attorney again this morning. There won't be any charges filed against you. It was a clean shoot, Rex."

Hearing that there would be no charges brought against me didn't make me feel any better. I had killed a man. Two days earlier I had walked in on my first dead body, and today I was a killer.

"Are you still there?" Rance asked.

"Yeah … yeah, I'm still here."

"I just wanted to keep you posted," Rance said. "Are you going to be okay?"

"I'll be okay."

"All right, Rex. If you need anything, give me a call."

"I will." I hung up the phone.

"Everything okay?" Christine asked.

"Yeah," I said. "Everything is fine." I looked to Kevin. "The police say if it was okay to go into Edgar's apartment?"

"Yeah," Kevin said. "They said it was all clear."

"Okay," I said. "I'm going to head up and get started." I turned and went out the door.

The walk down the alley, down the hall, and the ride up in the elevator seemed to take a lot longer than usual; all I could think about was Delbert Haskell. I tried to justify his death. *He broke into my house*, I thought. *I was protecting my home. It wasn't me who killed him. He didn't die from my bullet; he died from an infection. It was the hospital's fault.* No matter how long those excuses swirled around in my head, it made no difference: it was me who killed that twenty-eight-year-old boy.

I pulled the key ring off my belt loop, but I didn't need it, Edgar's door was unlocked. I re-clipped the keys, and went in. I left the door open behind me. I don't know if I did that to help let out the stink, or because it just felt eerie being in there alone with the door shut. I poked my head slowly into the kitchen. I don't know what I was expecting to see. Of course they had removed Edgar's body, but everything else was the same. The wooden chair still lay broken in the path. The smear of blood was still on the edge of the countertop and down the front of the sink base.

Detective Rance said it looked like Edgar had tried to change a light bulb in the ceiling fixture. The old rickety chair couldn't support his weight, and when the leg broke, Edgar hit his head against the edge of the countertop, breaking his neck. Sounded good to me.

I looked around the apartment, wondering where to start. This was going to be a big project. Kevin had rented a twenty-yard dumpster, but it wouldn't be here for a couple of days. He had spoken to the owner of the vacant lot behind Robinson Jewelry and gotten permission to bring the dumpster in from Third Street. I would be able to throw a lot of Edgar's stuff out a rear window, but it wouldn't land anywhere near the dumpster, which meant I would be handling everything twice. Yup, big job.

Someone behind me said, "Hey."

I almost shit myself. "Jesus Christ!" I said, spinning around. It was Kevin. "Don't do that!"

"A little jumpy, aren't we?" Kevin said with a grin.

"A little."

"Did you think it was Edgar's ghost?" He chuckled.

"I don't believe in ghosts," I shot back.

"That scream said otherwise."

"It wasn't a scream."

"Pretty damn close."

"What're you doing up here anyway?"

"Just wanted to see how you were making out."

"I just got up here." I pulled the lid off a forty-gallon plastic tote. Inside were about fifty cans of unopened tuna. "Hungry?"

"I don't think so," Kevin replied. He yanked the lid off of another tote. Inside that one was ten or fifteen containers of Nestle's Quik. The containers were the old cardboard ones, so they had been around for a while. The moisture in the air had caused the containers to swell over the years. "Wow."

"Am I supposed to save any of this stuff?" I asked. "Maude mentioned that Edgar had a brother named Everette. You think he'll want any of this furniture?"

"I can't imagine he would. He'll never get the stink out of it."

"You know how to get a hold of Everette?"

"Haven't seen or heard from him since the day he moved out. I mentioned him to Detective Rance. He said he would do his best to track him down."

"Maude said he moved out about three years ago."

"Yeah, three years sounds about right."

"They ever have jobs?"

"Everette never had a job that I can remember, but Edgar used to do odd jobs around town for some of the older folks. Mow lawns, rake leaves, things like that. He didn't seem to do too much after his brother moved out. That's around the time he started becoming more of a recluse."

"That when he became a hoarder?"

"No. The two of them were always like that."

We talked about Edgar and his brother for a few more minutes and then I changed the subject. "You say the roll-off will be here on Thursday?" I asked.

"Yeah," answered Kevin.

"Until then I'll try to straighten up the living room the best I can and move everything from the kitchen into the living room so I can fix the drainpipe."

"Sounds good," Kevin said. He turned and walked out of the kitchen. "Have fun."

"Yeah, thanks."

I followed the skinny pathway that ran between the stacks of junk and garbage through the dining room and into the living room. I spent the next two hours moving stuff around and re-stacking it higher and neater to make more room. When I had done all I could do in the living room, I began moving things from the dining room into the living room.

By the time most of the kitchen was cleared out, it was after one o'clock. I thought about running somewhere and grabbing lunch. I had worked in the apartment long enough that I could no longer smell the stench, but I wondered if others would be able to smell it on me if I went in somewhere to eat. I decided to work through lunch.

It took another two hours to cut out the broken section of pipe. I put a flexible Fernco coupling on the end of each cut section of cast iron pipe, and stuck a piece of PVC between them. I squirted a little clear silicone inside the Ferncos for good measure. I'd let the silicone dry overnight and then check for leaks in the morning.

I stepped back and admired my work. When I had my construction business I would have cut out the entire cast iron drain and replaced it. It would have taken a lot longer and cost a lot more, but that's not the way Kevin likes things done. He likes the best job I can do at the cheapest price.

I took a few steps back and sat down in the old wooden chair. I had positioned it upright earlier, forgetting it had a broken leg. The chair went back and I tumble ass over teakettle to the floor, hitting my head on the linoleum. "Dammit," I said, to no one in particular.

I sat on my butt staring at the broken chair while rubbing the back of my head. I instinctively looked at my fingertips for blood. Of course there wasn't any; I hadn't hit the floor hard enough. I guess I was a lot luckier than Edgar. I moved my neck around. Nope, not broken.

I had once read somewhere about a haunted rocking chair. Somewhere in England, I think it was. Everyone who sat in the chair later died a horrible death. I wondered if Edgar was just unlucky enough to end up with a haunted chair. I didn't believe in such things, but the chair would surely be the first thing to go into the dumpster, just to be on the safe side.

I got up from the floor and picked up the chair. There was a big smear of blood on the bottom of the seat. I was sure it was Edgar's blood. The sight of it made my skin crawl a bit. I carried the chair into the living room and placed it in the corner where I couldn't see it. *Your days are numbered, chair*, I thought.

I left Edgar's apartment around three, locked up, and headed downstairs.

"Kevin around?" I asked. "Oops, I said *Kevin* again."

"He already left for the day," Mark said.

"Okay. If you see him later, tell him I repaired the drain pipe. I squirted some silicone inside the Ferncos, so I'm going to wait until tomorrow to check for leaks."

"Sounds good," Mark responded.

"I'm going home." I turned and started for the door.

"Hey," Mark said.

I turned back. "Yeah?"

Mark looked around the store for listening ears. "I heard Delbert Haskell died yesterday."

"Yup," I said. I waited for more, but he didn't say anything else. I knew he wanted to say something like "Don't let it bother you," or "Hang in there," or something to that effect. After a few seconds I nodded my head and went out the door.

Chapter Eleven

Gayle and I sat at a booth at Pepper's Mexican Grill. Gayle ordered the enchiladas rancheros. I ordered the chicken chimichanga. We sipped our margaritas and ate chips and salsa while we waited for our meals to arrive.

"He was a scumbag," Gayle said.

"That doesn't make me feel any better," I told her.

"He broke into our house and he had a weapon."

"I know."

"You said he moved toward you with a knife."

"He did."

"Then you had no other option."

"Like I said, that doesn't make me feel any better."

"Anyone else would have done the same thing."

"Maybe."

Gayle reached across the table and placed her hand on top of mine. "I know it's difficult. My first kill—"

"Your *first* kill?"

"Listen, you can't let this consume you," Gayle said. "You did what you had to do. It's not your fault Haskell chose to break into our house that night."

"I know."

"You shot him in the leg, for Chrissakes. What were the odds he would get an infection and die?"

"I know."

"Everything's going to be okay."

"Unless his brothers—"

"We'll cross that bridge *if* we come to it."

I took another sip of my drink and then rubbed the back of my head. There was a pretty good lump back there from my tumble in Edgar's apartment.

"What's the matter?" Gayle asked. She scooped salsa out of the small bowl with a corn chip.

"The matter?" I asked.

"Why are you rubbing your head?"

"Oh, I sat in a broken chair in Edgar's apartment, fell backwards, and hit my head on the floor. There's just a little lump; no blood."

"You gotta be more careful."

"It was the same chair Edgar fell from and hit his head."

"Bad chair."

"Yeah," I agreed. "His blood was still under the seat. It gave me the heebie-jeebies."

"*Under* the seat?" Gayle asked.

"Yeah."

"I thought you said he hit his head on the edge of the counter top."

"He did."

"Then how did his blood get on the bottom of the chair?"

"I don't know. Maybe it splashed under there."

"Splashed?" Gayle asked.

"Sprayed?" I offered.

"How much blood was there?"

"On the chair?"

"No, on the floor … where he lay."

"There was a little pool of it under his head."

"Did you see blood anywhere else?"

"There was some on the counter top—where Rance says he hit his head when he fell—and a smear of it down the front of the sink base."

"Was there blood spatter anywhere else? Did you see any on the walls, or on the ceiling?"

"I didn't notice any."

91

"Huh."

"Why?"

"I don't know, just thinking out loud."

"What *exactly* are you thinking?"

"Just seems odd."

"What seems odd?"

"The blood on the bottom of the chair."

"You want me to mention it to Rance?"

Gayle chuckled. "Yeah," she said sarcastically, "he would love that. Don't say anything about it."

The waiter arrived and set our plates in front of us. "Here ya go," he said. "Is there anything else I can get for you?"

I looked around the table for some hot sauce, and saw it next to the salt and pepper shakers, behind Gayle's purse. "I don't think so," I said.

"I'm good," said Gayle.

The young Hispanic waiter grinned and nodded his head. "Enjoy." He turned and went back through the swinging cafe doors to the kitchen.

"I scooped up a forkful of refried beans and shoved them into my mouth. "Mm-mm good."

Gayle cut into one of her enchiladas and the steam rose up from the tortilla.

"Well, well, look who it is," said someone behind me.

Gayle looked up from her plate, and I turned to see a large bearded man moving around to the end of our table. He was over six foot tall and weighed at least 260. He wore jeans, a white T-shirt, and work boots. He was smiling, but the extreme anger in his crazy eyes said he was not happy. I didn't recognize the man.

"Beau Haskell," Gayle whispered to me across the table.

Beau's focus moved from me to Gayle, then back to me. "You're the piece ah shit that killed my little brother."

I looked around the room to see if anyone was watching.

"That's right," said Gayle.

Beau's eyes darted to Gayle, and then back. "You let your woman speak for you?" he sneered.

"No," I said. I started to rise up from my seat. Beau put his hand on my shoulder, shoving me back down.

Gayle slid to the edge of the booth and brought her foot up over the table and gave Beau a swift kick in the balls with her heel.

Beau let out a sound that was half moan and half grunt. He took a few steps back and grabbed his crotch. "You bitch!" he shouted.

Gayle was up and out of the booth like lightning. She squared off in front of Beau, and then leapt into the air. Doing a complete three-sixty, she gave Beau a spinning back kick to the side of the head.

The big man didn't go down, but he did sidestep a few feet, and when he turned back toward Gayle he had the dazed look of an old palooka about to hit the canvas.

I was out of my seat and moving toward Beau. I hit him once in the jaw with a right, and then a left to the ribs.

Beau brought up his arm and caught me in the shoulder, sending me flying across the dining room. I skidded on my belly across the slick floor and smashed headfirst into a busboy's cart. Now everyone in the room was watching. I heard a woman scream and a few people shouted. I quickly got back to my feet to see Beau moving toward Gayle with his gorilla arms outstretched.

Gayle took a step back and reached into her purse. She yanked out her .38 snub nosed revolver and jammed it into Beau's gut. Beau froze, and so did I. The room went silent.

"You so much as blink your eyes," Gayle warned, "and I'll tell this thing to open you up."

Beau didn't blink.

"You understand me?" Gayle asked.

Beau was afraid to nod his head.

"Now you back the hell up and get your redneck ass outta here."

Beau started slowly backing away toward the door.

"If you *ever* come near my husband or me again, I'll part your head like Moses parted the Red Sea."

The room remained quiet the whole time Gayle kept the gun in her hand. When Beau was gone and the door shut behind him, Gayle slipped the .38 back into her purse, and sat back down. "I'm starving," she said.

"Yeah, me too," I said.

The restaurant filled with chatter, but Gayle and I ignored it.

I called the waiter over. "Can I get another margarita here?" I asked. "And bring another one for Wyatt Earp too."

Chapter Twelve

I walked into Edgar's apartment a little after nine on Wednesday morning; this time I closed the door behind me. When I got to the kitchen, I flipped on the light switch. I hadn't tried it the day before. The ceiling fixture lit up, but it didn't seem to make much of a difference. Luckily there was a window over the kitchen sink that let in enough light for me to work. I walked over to the countertop and inspected the bloodstain. I looked around the room for more of what Gayle had referred to as blood spatter; there wasn't any.

I went into the living room and got the broken chair and brought it back into the kitchen with me. I placed it under the ceiling light. I pushed it over so it was lying like I found it. I glanced over at the blood stain and then back at the chair.

There was a knock at the door and I heard the creak of the hinges.

"Rex?" Detective Rance called out.

"Yeah," I answered. "In here."

I was still standing in the middle of the kitchen when Rance entered. "Getting the place cleaned up, I see," he commented.

"Yup."

His eyes went to the chair. "What are you doing?"

"Nothing. What's up?"

"I heard there was a little commotion at Pepper's last night."

"Yup."

"You want to tell me what it was all about?"

"How did you hear about it?"

"I'm the police. When somebody pulls a gun on someone, we usually hear about it."

"Are you here to arrest me?"

"No. It wasn't you who pulled the gun."

"No."

"Tell me what happened."

"Beau Haskell showed up at our table."

"And?"

"There were words said, and one thing led to another."

"Did he threaten you or your wife?"

"Well—"

"Did he?"

"He put his hands on me first."

"So Gayle pulled a gun on him?"

"She kicked him in the nuts first," I explained. "She was protecting me."

"How gallant of her."

"Did you question anyone else who was there?"

"There was no need. No one filed a complaint. I'm just following up a lead."

"A lead?"

"More of a rumor."

"So … gossip."

"More or less."

"He was there to start something. We just started something first."

Rance walked from the kitchen into the dining room. "How much does an apartment like this go for?" he asked.

"I'm not sure," I replied. "You would have to ask Kevin."

"How long you think it will take to get it ready to rent?"

"With the hours I put in … maybe three weeks."

"Because you don't work Mondays and Fridays."

I grinned. "Exactly."

"Must be nice."

"You looking for an apartment, Rance?"

"My nephew is."

Rance walked around looking the place over for another few minutes and said, "I'm gonna take off. You think you can stay out of trouble for a while?"

"That's something you would have to ask the Haskell boys."

"I will." Rance turned and started down the hall.

I knew I shouldn't, and Gayle had warned me not to, but I did it anyway. "Wait a second, Rance."

He reversed and stuck his head back into the kitchen. "What is it?"

"There's blood on the bottom of Edgar's broken chair." I pointed down where the chair lay.

Rance pursed his lips and gave me one of those *who cares* looks. "So?"

"Well, if he was standing on the chair and the leg broke, he would have fallen forward and hit his head here." I pointed to the blood on the sink base. "The chair fell back there. How would there be blood on the bottom of the chair?"

"What are you trying to say?"

"I don't know. It just seems odd that his blood would have hit the bottom of the chair when there's no spatter anywhere else."

Rance gave me the most condescending look I had ever received in my life. "Spatter?" he asked.

"Blood spatter."

"Yeah, I know what spatter is."

"Well, don't you think it's kinda strange?"

"I'll tell you what, Rex, you leave the police work to me, and I'll leave the handyman work to you. Okay?" He turned and started back down the hall.

"The bulb in the ceiling light works, so I don't think he was changing it," I called out.

"Maybe he had already changed it," Rance hollered back, and went out the door.

"Maybe," I whispered to myself. "Maybe not."

Why did Gayle have to put that in my head? I wondered. *She knows how I am.* Over the next few hours, as I washed walls and caulked cracks in molding, I came up with at least five different scenarios in which someone broke into Edgar's apartment and murdered him. In not one of those scenarios did I come up with a reason why. I was sure no one broke in looking for his stash of Hidden Valley ranch dressing, or his plastic treasure chest full of Nestles Quik.

Broke in, I thought. I laid down my caulking gun, pulled out my cell phone, and dialed Gayle's number.

"What's up?" she answered.

"Hey, it's me," I said. "You busy?"

"Kinda. What do you need?"

"I was just wondering. What signs would I look for to determine if there had been a break in?"

"Our house!" Gayle gasped.

"No, Edgar's apartment."

"You were just standing around wondering that?"

"While I was working," I added.

"Well, sometimes there's damage to the door near the cylinder, or maybe damage to the doorjamb near the strike plate."

I walked down the hall as Gayle spoke. When I got to the door I opened it and examined the places Gayle mentioned. There was no damage to either, other than normal wear and tear.

"It doesn't really look like anything is damaged," I told her. "There's some scarring on the strike plate, but that's normal. There's no damage to the door."

"So, then there was probably no break-in," Gayle offered.

"Yeah," I agreed. "I'm probably just letting my imagination get the best of me."

"However," said Gayle, "it could have been someone with a lock picking kit, or someone he knew."

"Edgar knew everyone in town, so—hey, are you busting my balls?"

Gayle chuckled. "A little bit. Now get back to work, Colombo." She hung up and so did I.

"Lock picking kit," I grumbled.

Chapter Thirteen

I worked until a little after one on Wednesday afternoon. On my way home I stopped at the Publix on Sadler Road and picked up some hamburger meat, a tub of cottage cheese, and the largest bag of potato chips I could find. The bag said party size, but I knew Gayle and I would empty that bag by seven o'clock. I also grabbed a jug of margarita mix for Gayle and a two-liter bottle of ginger ale for me.

I walked out of Publix and crossed the parking lot to my truck. I put the two grocery bags on the seat and shut the door. Then I went next door to Amelia Liquor and grabbed a bottle of tequila and a bottle of Bacardi rum.

As I walked back to the truck with my booze in hand, the same black Jeep Cherokee that was sitting out in front of my house on Sunday morning drove slowly through the parking lot, between me and my truck. The driver stared at me as he passed by. I didn't recognize him, but when he raised his right hand and pointed his finger at me and mocked the firing of a pistol, I figured it was Bobby Joe Haskell, the other brother of Delbert Haskell. After he faked recoil, he pretended to blow smoke away from the tip of his finger. He grinned eerily at me and sped off. For a second there, I wished I carried a purse with a .38 revolver inside.

I got back to my truck and unlocked the door. Before climbing in I scanned the parking lot for more Haskells. I didn't see any, so I got in and drove away.

On the drive home I toyed with the idea of carrying my gun with me when I went somewhere. I know guys who did, but I just wasn't one of them. I had had that 9mm for over twenty years and had never taken it anywhere other than the shooting range. I always told myself I wasn't that paranoid, but now, with the Haskell issue, I wondered if it was time.

Gayle had always carried a pistol. Sometimes she carried it in her purse, and sometimes she carried it in an ankle holster she had. She even had a garter holster she wore around her thigh for those special occasions, like weddings and funerals, when she had to wear a dress. I didn't see Gayle as being paranoid when she carried her weapon. She was a retired cop, and most of them still carry. I guess I saw Gayle as a trained professional.

Maybe I should just take my gun out of the lock box in the closet and put it in the nightstand. That way I could get to it in hurry if I had to. That's where

Gayle keeps hers, not that she's ever had to retrieve it in a hurry. I did need it in a hurry when Delbert Haskell broke into our house, but I had completely forgotten hers was there, and went for mine instead. Those few extra seconds could have meant the difference between life and death. My death, of course, not Delbert's. At this point it didn't matter to him which gun I used. He was dead either way. Yeah, that's what I'll do; put it in the nightstand.

Chapter Fourteen

I made a pitcher of margaritas and brought it and a margarita glass out to the garage. A few years earlier I had turned the garage into a family room. There were two old couches, my old recliner, a coffee table, a couple end tables with lamps, and a TV, arranged on a 15x15 area rug. I had built removable screen inserts for the garage door opening that I took out in the winter, when we weren't using the family room.

I don't really know why we still called it a family room. Now that our son, Ben, had moved away, it was just the two of us. Not a very big family. Gayle and I hoped to be grandparents someday, but Ben and his girlfriend were too new in their relationship to be talking about that.

The walls of the garage were exposed studs and the ceiling was exposed trusses. Underneath the area rug was concrete painted dark gray. I had long planned to build a small bar with bar stools in one corner, but had just never gotten around to it.

"What," Gayle asked, "no salt on the rim?" She relaxed on the couch directly across from the television with her legs pulled up under her. The bag of potato chips I had purchased earlier was open and sitting on the cushion beside her.

I handed her the empty glass and then filled it. I set the pitcher on the coffee table in front of her. "Did you want salt?" I asked. I reached into the bag and pulled out a handful of chips.

"No. I just wanted to complain about something."

"It's hard to find things to complain about when you have such an awesome husband, isn't it?"

"Yes." Gayle sipped her margarita. "Perfect," she said.

"Me or the margarita?"

"The margarita."

"Did you expect anything less?" I returned to the kitchen to make my own drink.

When I returned with my Bacardi and ginger ale, I paused to survey the neighborhood through the screen. I took small sips of my drink as I looked down the driveway, around the cul-de-sac, and down Taurus Court. To my left, Glenn Simon had mowed half of his lawn and was now squatting down next to the mower fiddling with something. I knew if he couldn't get it started again, he would be over to borrow mine.

To my right, Chester Gable and his wife, Ho, were sitting in their driveway in lawn chairs. Each had a can of Keystone Light in their hand. Ho's full name was Chung Ho ... something or other, but everyone, including Chester, just called her Ho. They were nice people. They sat in their driveway most nights and had a few beers. Sometimes Gayle and I joined them, and sometimes they sat with us in our family room. Chester and Ho were in their mid-sixties. Chester was retired from the military, and Ho worked part-time at First Federal Bank of Florida.

Gayle and I were the youngest couple in the cul-de-sac. Even though we were in our forties, the neighbors referred to us as "the kids." Gayle liked that a lot.

"You going to start those burgers?" Gayle asked. "I'm getting hungry."

"*Getting* hungry?" I joked. "When aren't you hungry?" I turned around to see Gayle's reaction to my ribbing. She had just shoved a fistful of potato chips into her mouth and was pouring herself another margarita.

I turned and walked over to the gas grill, took hold of the handle, and wheeled it out the screen door into the driveway. I turned on the gas and hit the starter button ten or fifteen times. I knew it wasn't going to work, it never works. I shut off the gas and went in search of matches or a lighter.

When I returned to the garage, Glenn was standing in the middle of the room speaking with Gayle. He had a few potato chips that he was eating one at a time in the palm of his hand.

"Can't get her started?" I asked.

"Piece of shit," Glenn replied, shaking his head.

"Maybe it's time to get a new one," I suggested.

"I should just hire someone to do it."

"There's always that."

"Can I borrow yours?"

"Sure. You want a drink first?"

Glenn looked back over his shoulder toward his own house. He had that look on his face like he was about to break one of mom's rules. "Yeah, I got time for a quick one."

"What'll you have?"

He craned his neck. "Whaddaya got there, Gayle?" He eyeballed Gayle's drink like a red-tailed hawk eyes a field mouse.

"A margarita," said Gayle.

Glenn patted his stomach. "No." he said, "Those bother my stomach. What's that, Rex?"

"Bacardi and ginger ale," I said.

"That sounds good. I'll have one of those."

I went back into the kitchen to make Glenn's drink. *Yeah*, I thought, *I gotta build that bar*.

I returned to the garage and handed Glenn his drink. He tipped it up and chugged half the glass. "Ahh," he said. "I needed that." He stretched his neck to get a better look at his house through the screen.

"What are you looking for?" I asked.

"The old lady," Glenn replied. "I'm not supposed to be drinking at all." He grinned slyly. The small blood vessels in his cheeks and nose were broken. When he smiled his eyes almost closed completely.

"Why not?" Gayle asked.

"Oh, they ran one of those cameras down my throat and took a look in my belly. Said I got ulcers. Doctor said I'm a mess in there. Put me on some medication ... carrot something."

"Carafate?" Gayle asked.

"Yeah, that's it." Glenn downed the rest of his drink in his second gulp. "You got any gum or anything?"

"No," I said.

"Aw, never mind," he said. He grabbed my lawnmower by the handle and rolled it out through the screen door. "Y'all have a nice night."

"You too," Gayle said.

I stood at the screen watching Glenn as he rolled the lawnmower across the street and into his own yard. He pulled the starter cord once and it fired up. I glanced over at the Gables' place.

Chester raised his can of beer and shouted, "Evenin', neighbor!"

I raised my glass to him.

"Burgers," said Gayle.

"Oh yeah," I replied.

I made the burgers and we ate them in front of the television along with the cottage cheese, and the rest of the potato chips. When I finished my plate I put it on the coffee table, leaned back, and put my feet up on the table next to my plate. I laced my fingers behind my head and stared at the Judge Judy show. I hated Judge Judy, but Gayle was enthralled.

"The old bastard should be shot," Gayle said. She wasn't looking at me, so I assumed she was giving advice to Judy.

Seems the old guy bought a car for an eighteen-year-old girl, and now she didn't want to pay him back. She said it was a gift. I knew why the old guy bought her the car. Gayle knew why the old guy bought her the car. Judge Judy sure as hell knew why. But the old guy claimed they were just friends—you know, because all old guys have an eighteen-year-old female friends—and that he just loaned her the money for the car.

"Dirty old man," Gayle commented.

Both of us heard the throaty rev of a car engine and looked out through the screen panels. There was the black Jeep Cherokee sitting sideways at the end of our driveway. The engine revved again. I got up from my seat and so did Gayle. I walked toward the door.

"Don't go out there," Gayle said. I ignored her.

I went through the door and let it slam shut behind me. "Stay inside," I said.

I walked a few steps down the driveway. The driver revved the engine again. I could see Bobby Joe Haskell in the passenger seat. The window lowered.

"Your days are numbered, Langley!" he shouted.

I scanned the cul-de-sac. Glenn Simon and the Gables had all gone inside by then.

"Then come on, you redneck piece of shit!" I yelled back.

Bobby Joe laughed and spit a syrupy brown puddle of Red Man on my driveway.

"All in good time, Langley!"

I walked toward the Jeep.

The back tires spun and smoke swirled out from under the rear fenders. The ass end of the Jeep slid around, kicking gravel and dust toward me. I looked at the ground around me for something to throw. I saw a rock about the size of a golf ball and picked it up. As the Jeep started down the street, I let the rock fly, hitting the roof.

The driver slammed on the brakes. The reverse lights came on, but the Cherokee just sat there. I knew they were discussing whether or not to come back and kick the shit out of me. Part of me wanted them to keep going, but the other part wanted to get it over with.

After thirty or forty seconds the reverse lights went off, the tires spun, and away the Haskells went. Gayle joined me in the driveway as the Jeep rounded the corner onto Caprice Lane.

"I called the police," Gayle said. "This has got to end."

"It will," I assured her. "One way or another."

Chapter Fifteen

By the time Detective Rance got to our house there were already two patrol cars there. Gayle and I stood in the driveway with two uniformed officers. One asked questions and jotted down our answers in a notepad as we spoke. The other officer just stood there with his arms folded across his puffed up chest. We gave them Bobby Joe Haskell's name, but said we didn't see the driver, even though it was a sure bet it was his brother, Beau. We told the officers the make, model, and color of the vehicle. I told them about what happened in the Publix parking lot earlier in the day. Gayle was a little pissed that I had kept it from her.

Rance walked up the driveway toward us.

"Detective," the note-taker acknowledged him.

Rance nodded. "What did you do now?" he asked.

Puffy Chest started to speak but Rance halted him with the raise of a hand. "I want to hear it from the Rex's mouth," he said.

"It was Bobby Joe Haskell and his brother," I said.

"You pull a gun on him this time?" Rance asked.

"I didn't have one on me," I said.

"Too bad. You could have shot him in the leg."

"I should have shot him in the head," said Gayle.

The officers exchanged a look of bafflement and awe.

"Keep that to yourself," said Rance. "Did he threaten either one of you?"

"Not in so many words," I replied.

"How many words was it?"

"I said, 'Come on you redneck piece of shit,' and he hollered back, 'All in good time.'"

"Yeah, not really a threat," said Rance.

"But we know what he meant," Gayle said.

"Yeah, we know," Rance agreed. "That Bobby Joe is a tough son of a bitch. He did six years in Raiford for involuntary manslaughter."

"Involuntary?" I asked.

"That was the plea," said Rance.

"So what do we do now," I asked, "just sit around and wait for them to strike?"

"Maybe we should strike first," said Gayle.

"Stop that talk," Rance scolded. "You know I can't have you out there making things worse."

"But if we strike first," Gayle said, "then it'll be worse for them and not us."

"And that's the way I would rather it be," I added.

"I'll go out there tonight and have a talk with them, let them know we're watching them."

"You think that'll help?" I asked.

"Probably not," Rance responded. "But it's worth a try."

The officer closed his notepad and put it back in his breast pocket, and slid his pen in next to it. "We all done here?" he asked.

"Why don't the two of you drive by a few times tonight," Rance suggested.

"Roger that," said Puffy Chest.

Both officers walked down the driveway to their units and drove away. When Rance headed for his car I followed; Gayle turned and went back inside the garage.

"I feel pretty helpless just sitting here like this … waiting for them to come back," I told Rance.

"I know," he said, climbing into his car. "But until one of them does something illegal, our hands are tied."

I stood at the end of the driveway and watched Rance's car until he rounded the corner. I glanced over at Chester's place; he was watching out his front window. He let the curtain drop when he caught me looking. I turned my head toward Glenn's; he was also watching out his window. He gave me a half wave. I waved back.

When I moved back toward the house I saw Chester out of the corner of my eye. He was now standing at his open front door. "Everything okay, neighbor?" he called out.

"Yeah, Chester, everything is fine." I gave him a wave as well

"Why didn't you tell me you saw Bobby Joe at Publix?" Gayle asked, when I got back inside.

"Because I didn't want to worry you." I walked over and picked up the bag of potato chips and reached inside. "Empty," I griped.

"Great," Gayle said, on her way into the house. "Why does everything bad happen to us?"

I snickered.

Chapter Sixteen

Later that night I shut off the television and closed the living room curtains. I went into the dining room, and then the kitchen, making sure every window and door was locked tight. We had a three-foot piece of an old broom handle that laid in the track of the sliding glass door. We usually didn't use it and just left it standing against the jamb, but I was feeling extra cautious in light of the recent bullshit, and dropped into the track. I jiggled the door, making sure it was secure. I wondered if my window alarms had come in yet.

I walked back to the living room, stepped over Delbert's bloodstain, and went down the hall. I checked the windows in Ben's old bedroom and the spare bedroom, and joined Gayle in our bedroom.

Gayle was sitting at the edge of the bed. She had her revolver in her hand with the cylinder open. She slowly spun the cylinder with her thumb.

"Locked and loaded?" I joked. I was just as nervous as Gayle, but I wasn't about to let her know that.

"You can never be too ready," she replied. She closed the cylinder and placed the .38 in her nightstand drawer.

I hadn't told Gayle, but my 9mm was also in my nightstand drawer.

Gayle swung her legs into bed and pulled the covers over her. I took off my pants and got into bed. We both lay there on our backs staring at the slowly spinning ceiling fan above us.

"How was work today?" Gayle asked.

"Good," I replied.

"How long you think it will take you to get the apartment ready to rent?"

"A few weeks. Rance said his nephew was looking for an apartment. I told him to talk to Kevin about it."

"Huh."

"I mentioned to Rance what you said about the blood on the bottom of Edgar's chair."

"I told you not to say anything."

"I didn't tell him it was your theory."

"Theory?" Gayle asked. "I didn't have a *theory*."

"Well, I didn't tell him you were wondering."

"I wasn't wondering either. I just mentioned it."

"It seemed to me like you were wondering."

"Well, I wasn't. What did he say?"

"See, you were wondering."

"I am now."

"I asked him how he thought the blood got underneath the chair if Edgar fell forward and hit his head on the counter top. I mentioned that if he went forward, and the chair went in the other direction, and there was no blood spatter anywhere else in the room, how did the blood get there? I also let him know that the light bulb in the kitchen wasn't blown."

"What did he say?"

"He said that I should stick to maintenance work and leave the police work to him."

Gayle chuckled. "That's good advice."

"Thanks."

"I'm joking," Gayle said apologetically.

"What do you think?" I asked. "You must have had something in mind, or you wouldn't have brought it up to begin with. What do you think happened?"

"I don't know. I would have had to see the crime scene."

"There wasn't much of a crime scene. There was Edgar dead on the floor, a chair with a broken leg, and blood on the edge of the countertop."

"And you said there was a small pool of blood on the floor, under Edgar's head."

"Yes."

"Well, first I would want to see the coroner's report to see if there were any other injuries."

"Why would there be other injuries?"

"If someone hit him in the back of the head with the chair."

"You think someone hit him in the back of the head with a chair?"

"It would be another way to explain the broken chair, *and* the blood underneath the seat."

"So you're thinking that someone hit him over the head with the chair, then he fell forward and hit his head on the counter top."

"No, I'm not thinking that. I was just throwing it out there."

"We have to get a look at that coroner's report."

"Go to sleep," Gayle said, and reached for the lamp switch.

"Are coroner's reports public records?"

"I'm not sure."

"How do we find out?"

"Go to sleep."

"Should I ask Rance?"

"Yeah, that would be a great idea."

"It probably wouldn't, would it?"

"Go to sleep."

Chapter Seventeen

Detective Rance stopped by Edgar's apartment again on Thursday, a little before lunch time. "How's things going in here?" he asked.

I had one of the bedroom windows open and was throwing junk out it to the ground below. "Since yesterday?" I asked. "Not much has changed."

Rance walked to the window and stuck his head through the opening. "Too bad you couldn't get the dumpster a little closer."

"Yup," I responded. "Too bad."

"You're going to have to handle everything twice."

I had heard about the legendary Captain Obvious, and now here he was, right in the apartment with me. "Yup." I stood behind him holding a cardboard box full of yarn, waiting for him to move. He finally did, and I threw the box through the opening.

"Throwing everything away, huh?" Rance asked.

"Almost everything," I replied. "Kevin said to keep any personal items that I thought his brother might want."

"Oh yeah," Rance said. "I got a hold of his brother Everette yesterday afternoon. He's living up in the Myrtle Beach area. He was pretty upset when he got the news."

"Did you tell him Edgar's funeral is tomorrow?"

"I told him."

"Is he going to make it?"

"He said he had no way to get here."

"That's awful. I feel bad for the poor guy."

"You could drive up there and pick him up."

"I don't feel that bad."

"I didn't think so."

"I guess I'll just put Edgar's personal belongings in one of the storerooms."

"Good idea."

"You talk to the Haskell's last night?"

"I did."

"What did they have to say?"

"I told them to stay away from your house or they could be charged with harassment. They assured me that they were just trying to throw a scare into you."

"I hope you didn't tell them it was working."

I kept throwing boxes out the window while Rance just stood there watching. I wondered if police work was boring in a city like Fernandina Beach. It probably was. I read the newspaper most mornings and it didn't seem to me like there was a lot of criminal activity.

Rance took a deep breath and exhaled. "Well, I better head out," he said.

"You have lunch yet?" I asked.

"Nope."

"How about I buy you lunch?"

"Why?"

"I want to pick your brain about something?"

"What about?"

"We'll talk about it at lunch."

"Okay, you can buy me lunch, but this doesn't mean we're going to be friends."

I flipped off the kitchen light and followed Rance down the hall. "You say that now, but once you get to know me, you won't be able to get enough of me."

"I've already had enough of you, and I've only known you for a few days."

I slapped him on the back. "What a kidder."

*****

Rance and I walked around the corner to The Crab Trap. Everyone we passed said either "Good afternoon, Detective," or "How's it going, Calvin?" Only two of the passersby knew me by name. It was easy to see from the expression on Rance's face that he enjoyed being recognized.

I pulled open the big wooden door and let Rance walk in first. After all, out of the two of us, he was the important one.

"You want to sit at the bar?" I asked.

Rance looked at his watch. "Better not," he said. "I'm still on duty."

I imagined Rance thought he was always on duty. We took a seat at the four top to the right of the door.

A young brunette hurried over. It probably threw her that we sat down even though the chalkboard sign in front of the door clearly told us to wait to be seated. It even said please. We were rebels, Rance and I.

"Good afternoon, gentlemen," she said. "Can I get you something to drink?"

"I'll have a Bacardi and ginger," I said.

"A Diet Coke for me, thanks," said Rance.

The waitress returned with our drinks a few minutes later and took our order. I got the Shrimp Po Boy, and Rance ordered a house salad with fat free dressing on the side. When the waitress walked away

I asked Rance if he was a health nut. He asked me what I meant by that. "Nothing," I said.

"So, what did you want to talk to me about?" Rance asked.

I didn't know exactly how to begin so I just ripped off the Band-Aid. "Was there an autopsy done on Edgar Hayes?"

Rance shook his head and rolled his eyes. "Why?" he asked.

"Gayle and I can't get past the blood on the bottom of the chair."

"Gayle and you?"

"Well, mostly Gayle." I figured I might as well throw Gayle under the bus since she wasn't there to defend herself. "She was a cop for twenty years, you know."

"I know."

"She wondered if there were any other wounds on Edgar's head. She thinks Edgar may have been hit over the head with the chair, and then hit his head on the countertop."

"She does, does she?" It was obvious Rance was a little perturbed with the conversation.

"Yeah."

"Did Gayle come up with a motive?" Rance asked. He fixed me in a stare that made me wish I hadn't even started.

"A motive?"

"Yeah, a motive. Why would anyone want Edgar Hayes dead? He had no enemies. He had no life insurance. He barely ever went out of that damn apartment. I bet most of the people in town thought he was already dead."

"You got a point there."

"Gee, ya think?"

"How do you think the blood got under the seat?"

"I don't know!"

Everyone in the place looked over at us. I grinned back at them nervously. "You don't have to yell."

The waitress arrived with our plates and set them in front of us. "Here you go," she said. "Y'all need anything else, just give a shout." We thanked her and she scurried away.

Rance stabbed his fork angrily into his salad and then dipped it into his fat free dressing.

I took a big bite out of my Po Boy. "How's that salad?" I asked.

"How do you think it is?" Rance shot back. "It's friggin' lettuce."

My neighbor, Glenn, used to be a pretty big boozer, but now he wasn't supposed to drink at all, and a tough guy like Detective Calvin Rance was drinking a Diet Coke and eating salad with fat free dressing. What was the world coming to? I didn't know, but I didn't like it.

We sat there eating and not saying a word to each other. I wondered if Rance was right, and we weren't going to be friends. After a few more minutes, Rance said quietly, "I'll check on that autopsy report."

"Thanks, pal," I replied.

"We're not pals," he said.

"Not yet," I responded with a big grin.

Chapter Eighteen

Friday afternoon Gayle and I stood at Edgar's graveside at the Bosque Bello Cemetery. It was a cool, cloudy day. The forecast was for rain, but we hadn't seen any. We stood under an old oak tree that was covered in Spanish moss. There were a lot of trees covered in moss. I wondered if Edgar would like being buried here, or if he would prefer something more cluttered.

Kevin Collins was there, and so were three or four of Edgar's neighbors. In spite of never meeting Edgar, Reverend Martin gave him a nice eulogy. Mostly he just stated facts that Kevin and I provided ahead of time, but he did it in a way that sounded like he knew the man his entire life. It was nice, and the reverend's voice was very calming. Almost calming enough to make me think about going to his church … almost.

Just as the cemetery workers began lowering Edgar's casket into the ground, Detective Rance walked up beside me.

"Nice little service," Rance said. "I wouldn't think he could afford something like this."

"Kevin put a donation jar by the cash register," I replied. "That took care of some of it. Gayle and I, and Kevin and his wife, split the difference."

"Seriously?"

"Yeah."

"Huh. That was pretty nice of you guys."

"What are ya gonna do?"

"Thank you, everyone, for coming," Reverend Martin said. He stayed at the graveside until the rest of us walked back to our cars.

Rance walked with Gayle and me. "I took a look at the coroner's report," he said.

"Anything suspicious?" I asked.

"No," Rance replied.

Gayle continued to walk with us, but pretended to pay no attention to the conversation. That's how Gayle is. She's of the mindset that if no one realizes you're listening, then they didn't know what you knew.

I felt as though Rance was holding something back. "But?" I prompted.

"But what?"

"But you did find something."

"He had a gash over his right eye."

"I knew it!" I said, just a little too loud. "You were right, Gayle."

Gayle gave me a slight grin and winked.

"I didn't notice the cut over his eye because of the blood from the other wound." Rance sounded almost apologetic. "The cut on his forehead and the cut over his eye were so close, it looked like one wound."

We stopped at my truck. "What now?" I asked.

"The coroner is still ruling it an accidental death," said Rance. "So nothing next."

"Someone hit him with that chair, Rance," I said.

"Slim chance," Rance replied.

"A slim chance is better than no chance," Gayle offered.

"Not for Edgar," I said. "That slim chance got him killed."

"Falling off a chair got him killed," said Rance.

"Maybe," I said.

"Maybe not," said Gayle.

"I'm sticking with maybe," Rance said. "That is, unless you two amateur sleuths come back with a little more than a blood stain on the bottom of a chair seat."

"Something more like what?" I asked.

"Something more like"—Rance held up his hand and counted to three with his fingers—"means, motive, and opportunity. You two have a nice day off." He turned and walked back to his car.

"Why's he gotta be like that?" I asked.

"Cops don't like to change their minds," Gayle replied. "It's like admitting they're wrong."

"But he might be wrong." I opened the passenger side door for Gayle and she climbed in. I watched as the slit in her black skirt slid to the side and revealed her thigh and some of her butt cheek. I always opened the door for Gayle, but when she was wearing a skirt, I felt like she was saying thank you.

I walked around to the driver's side and got in. "I wish you had never mentioned anything," I said.

"About what?" Gayle asked.

"The damn blood on the bottom of the seat."

"You're the one who let it snowball."

"It's still your fault."

"Why do you say that?"

"Because you know how I am. You should have known better."

We drove slowly along the thin dirt pathway that wound through the cemetery. I looked over at another funeral that was taking place about a hundred yards off the path. There must have been sixty people at the gravesite. I wondered who he or she was. I thought about Delbert Haskell. I wondered when his funeral was. I wondered how many people would be standing around his grave site.

Chapter Nineteen

Saturday afternoon Gayle had to be to work by one, and I was bored as hell by one thirty. I walked out through the garage and down the driveway with two LandShark lagers in my hand. As I walked up Chester Gable's driveway I noticed his truck wasn't in the garage. *Dammit*, I thought. I decided to knock anyway. Who knows, maybe Ho took the truck somewhere.

I rapped on the front door a few times and waited.

Ho pulled the door open. "Hey, Rex," she said.

"Chester around?" I asked. I held up the bottles of beer.

"Sorry, Rex, he drove down to his brother's in Sanford. He probably won't be back until late this afternoon."

"Oh, okay," I said. "Sorry to bother you." I turned and headed back down the driveway. I was almost halfway across the cul-de-sac before I wondered if I should have offered Ho the beer. Then as I walked up Glenn's driveway, I wondered if he had seen me go to Chester's first, and knew he was my second choice.

I knocked on Glenn's door.

"Hey, buddy," said Glenn.

"Brought you a beer," I said, holding up one.

"*Shh!*" he said, with a finger to his lips. "I told ya, I ain't supposed to be drinking." He looked back over his shoulder for his wife. When he was certain she hadn't heard me, he stepped outside and pulled the door shut behind him.

I cowered. "Ooh, sorry," I said. "I forgot about that. You want me to get you a soda, or something?"

"Give me the damn beer," he said, yanking it from my hand, twisting off the cap, and taking a big swig. "Come on, let's go over to your garage."

"You want to put some shoes on first?" I asked.

"No."

Glenn hurried down his driveway and up mine. I walked fast to keep up with him. He was inside the garage first and plopped down on the couch. "Turn on the game," he said.

"Game?" I asked.

"Yanks and Rays," he said. "ESPN."

I grabbed the remote and tuned in. It was bottom of the second with one man on, Ramos was at bat and the count was one and one. Sabathia pitched a change up and Ramos swung. Glenn and I knew it was a home run the second it left his bat; so did everyone else watching the game.

Glenn cheered in his usual over-animated style, and I just shouted, "Yes!"

The Rays took the lead, five to four.

"Got another one of these?" Glenn asked.

"Are you sure?" I asked.

"Never been more sure of anything in my whole life, pal."

I went to the kitchen to get us both another one. Glenn wasn't supposed to be drinking, but he was a big boy, and I wasn't his mom, or his wife.

"Here ya go," I said, when I returned. I took a seat in my old recliner, but not before first grabbing the remote control. I had watched TV with Glenn on several occasions, and it didn't take me long to figure out he was a channel surfer. The second a commercial came on, Glenn was surfing from one station to another, sometimes forgetting to go back to the original program. I, on the other hand, put it on a channel and kept it there until the end. Sometimes that drove Glenn nuts. My house, my rules.

When the inning was over, and the game went to commercial, Glenn turned to me. "Why were the cops here the other day?" he asked. "Was it about the guy ya kilt?"

"It's a long story," I said.

"I ain't goin' nowhere."

"Before the cops came, did you see the Jeep Cherokee with two rednecks parked outside my driveway?"

"Nope."

"Well, that was Delbert Haskell's brothers."

"They harrasin' y'all?"

"They've just been driving by the house, and we also had a little run-in with the older one at a restaurant the other night."

"Sounds like they's just tryin' to intimidate ya. I wouldn't worry about it if I's you. Besides, you got that little lady of yers to protect ya." Glenn chuckled.

"What's that supposed to mean?" I shot back.

"You know."

"No, I don't know."

"She's kinda the tough one outta the two of y'all."

"I'm a half a foot taller than her and outweigh her by about seventy pounds," I argued.

"And yet she's the tough one."

"You're an asshole, Glenn."

"At least I wear the pants in my family."

"Chester!" someone shouted.

We both jumped. It was Chester's wife, Daisey. Her face was up against the screen panel, and she had fire in her eyes. Her fists were doubled and jammed into her giant love handles.

"What the hell do you think yer doin'!" she hollered. Her voice echoed through the garage. I don't know who had the greater look of fear, Glenn, or me.

"I ... uh," Glenn replied.

"I ... uh," Daisey aped, trying her best to look as foolish as Glenn.

"I was watchin' the game, sweetheart," said Glenn. His voice was shaky.

"What's that in yer hand?" she yelled.

Glenn showed his empty hand. "Nothin'."

"The other hand, stupid!"

"A beer."

"You set that bottle down and don't you take another sip!" she ordered. "Then you get your damn fool ass ta home."

"Yes, dear," said Glenn. He put the bottle on the coffee table and stood.

Daisey spun on her heels and stormed down the driveway. Her fists were still clenched.

"Yeah, Glenn," I said. "At least you wear the pants in your family."

"Shut up ... and I saw you walk over to Chester's first."

Chapter Twenty

On Sunday Gayle and I drove down to Jacksonville, to The Avenues Mall. Gayle shopped and I followed her around from store to store wishing I was doing anything other than walking around a mall. We had lunch at the Burger Barn, and then shopped some more.

After the shopping portion of our day was complete, we drove over to Jacksonville Beach and had dinner at Ocean Grille and Bar. I stuffed myself on steamed oysters and blackened grouper; best part of my day.

Gayle worked the lunch crowd on Monday, and I decided to go to work, even though I don't work on Mondays. When I got to Collins' Hardware, Kevin informed me that Detective Rance had stopped by a few minutes earlier, and was up in Edgar's apartment.

"He is, is he?" I asked. "What for?"

"He asked if he could go up and take a look around," Kevin replied.

"I'll go up and surprise him."

I stepped off the elevator onto the second floor and walked quietly down the hall to Edgar's apartment—I wondered how long I would refer to it as Edgar's apartment—and peeked in through the open door. I paused and listened. Nothing. I tiptoed as quietly as I could down the hall and stuck my head into the kitchen. There was Rance bent over the broken chair. He was sticking what looked to me like clear packing tape in spots all over the chair. There were a few pieces stuck to the seat, and a few on the back of the chair. Sitting next to Rance on the floor was a small metal toolbox with FINGERPRINT KIT written on the lid in black Sharpie.

I put my hands over my head, trying to imitate a ghost, and stepped into the doorway. "Woooo," I said.

Rance spun around and hit the floor. "Jesus!" he shouted.

I burst into laughter at the sight of sheer terror in his eyes. Would I have hated someone doing that to me? You bet your ass I would. But it was pretty damn funny doing it to someone else.

"Are you out of your goddamn mind!" Rance shouted.

I was doubled over and holding my stomach at that point. I felt like I might puke.

"I'm wearing a gun, for Chrissakes!" shouted Rance.

"I'm a ghost," I said through the laughter. "The bullet would have gone right through me."

Rance climbed to his feet. "Not funny."

"You should have been standing over here, because from here it was pretty damn funny."

The color was just coming back into Rance's face. "What are you doing here?" he demanded. "I thought you didn't work on Mondays."

"Hold on," I said, holding my belly. "My stomach hurts."

Rance waited for me to regain my composure.

"I just stopped in," I explained, "and Kevin said you were up here. What are you doing?"

Rance looked down at the chair. "I was just seeing if I could lift some prints off this thing."

I cocked my head and raised an eyebrow. "Oh, were you?"

"Shut up." Rance carefully peeled away the pieces of tape and stuck each one carefully onto a white piece of plastic. He opened the lid of the fingerprint kit and took out several small evidence bags and placed the prints inside.

"Got you thinking, didn't we?" I asked.

"I had nothing better to do," Rance grumbled. When he was finished he closed the lid of the kit and stood up. "I'm not expecting too much. Six or seven people have probably handled this chair.. You, me, the two paramedics, Edgar, Kevin, and anyone else who's been in here."

"It never hurts to try."

"It doesn't, huh? You know how much it costs to have prints sent to the FDLE and have them processed?"

"FDLE?" I asked.

"Florida Department of Law Enforcement."

"Why do you have to send them there?"

"Believe it or not, we don't have a crime scene lab here in Fernandina Beach."

"Oh. How much does it cost?"

"Well, I don't know exactly, but it's not free."

"How long's it take?"

"Probably a couple weeks."

"Weeks? Why does it take weeks?"

"I don't know, Rex. Maybe the FDLE doesn't work on Mondays and Fridays."

Chapter Twenty-One

I was dialing my cell phone before I even got back to my truck. "Hey, are you busy?" I asked.

"Well, it is right in the middle of lunch," Gayle said, "and I am a waitress, so …"

"Rance lifted fingerprints off the chair, and he's sending them to the FDLE." I knew I sounded way too excited, but hey, listen to me: I was saying things like "lifted" and "FDLE."

"That's great, baby," Gayle replied. She didn't sound anywhere near as excited as me. "I have to get back to work. I'm being glared at. Love ya."

"Love yo—"

Click.

I tossed the cell onto the seat next to me. *Two weeks*, I thought. *What do we do in the meantime?* I grabbed my cell again and dialed Rance's number.

"Rance," he answered, just like a cop in a cop show. There was no "Detective Rance speaking. How may I help you?" Nope, it was just, "Rance." Cool. I wondered if I should start answering my phone, "Langley."

"Hey, buddy. What's up?" I asked.

"What now?"

"I was wondering if you had lunch yet."

"Nope."

"You want to get lunch?"

"Nope. I'm going home for lunch."

"Why's that?"

"Because my wife wanted me to come home for lunch today."

"Oh."

"Anything else?"

"No."

Click.

Hmm, lunch alone. The bad thing about retiring in your late forties is that all your friends are still working. Everything you do during the day, like having lunch or going golfing, is either done alone, or with guys in their seventies.

I started the engine and put the old girl in drive. My cell started ringing so I shoved the gear shift back into park. I picked up the phone and read the caller ID; it was Glenn. *Yes!* I thought. *An old person.*

I tapped the call icon and said, "Langley."

"Rex?" Glenn asked.

"Yeah."

"Why did you answer the phone like that?"

"Like what?"

"Langley!"

"That's ... how I always answer my phone."

"No it's not. You usually say—"

"What do you want, Glenn?"

"Hey, remember that Jeep Cherokee?"

"Of course I remember it, Glenn. What about it?"

"It was here on the street again today."

"Dammit. What did they do?"

"The woman drove down the street and around the cul-de-sac real slow-like."

"It was a woman?"

"Yeah. Crazy, huh?"

"She was alone?"

"Yup. I took out my phone and took some pictures of her and a short video."

"Did she see you?"

"Yup. She flipped me the bird."

"Can you text me the pictures, Glenn?"

"Sure thing. I'll hang up and—"

"You don't have to hang up, Glenn just— Glenn?" He had hung up.

I waited for the pictures to arrive. They never came. My cell rang again.

"Hey, Glenn," I said.

"You get 'em?"

"No."

"Hold on."

"Don't hang up, Glenn, just—Glenn? Good God."

I put the truck back in drive and started down Centre Street. I answered my phone for the third time. "Hello, Glenn."

"How come you didn't say, 'Langley?'"

"I don't know."

"Did you get 'em?"

"I'm on my way home, Glenn."

"Okay. You eat lunch yet?"

"No."

"Good. Daisey made tuna salad."

"I'll be there in a bit."

"Can you sneak me over a beer?"

"No!"

I arrived home a few minutes later and pulled the truck into my driveway. Glenn was standing in his driveway. I knew he had been waiting there since he called me. He looked as excited about his cell phone pictures as I was about Rance lifting the prints. I guess deep down, everyone wishes they were a private detective like on television; guys, anyway. Women aren't that foolish.

Glenn met me about the halfway point and held the cell phone out to me. I took it and examined the photograph.

"Glenn," I said, "this is a picture of a Jeep Wrangler, and it's blue."

"Yeah, dark blue."

"The Cherokee was black … and it was a Cherokee."

"So you don't think that's the same vehicle?"

"No, Glenn. I'm pretty sure this blue Jeep Wrangler isn't the same vehicle as the black Jeep Cherokee."

"You think there's someone else out to get ya?"

"No, Glenn. I don't."

"Well, that's good. I hope you're hungry."

"I'm not really crazy about tuna salad."

"I already told Daisey you were coming over. She opened two cans."

"I don't know what you want me to say, Glenn."

"You better say yer comin' over for lunch."

"Okay."

"About that beer."

"No, Glenn."

Chapter Twenty-Two

By Wednesday I had gotten every bit of Edgar's crap loaded into the dumpster. Anything I thought his brother might someday want, I put in cardboard boxes and put them in one of the storerooms. There were three photo albums, a Bible, some old comic books I thought might be worth something, and some baseball cards. I saved two ashtrays that had the name Hayes engraved on the bottom. There were a few bowling, softball, and basketball trophies with Edgar's name on the nameplate. Who knew Edgar was once a jock? I wondered at what point in his life he took the wrong turn. Edgar's entire life was reduced to four boxes in the corner of a third floor storeroom.

When I had emptied the entire apartment—except for the broken wooden chair—I ripped up the carpeting in the living room and two bedrooms. I rolled up the carpeting and tossed it out the bedroom window.

After sweeping the entire place, and running my Shop-Vac around, I went downstairs to grab the twelve gallons of paint Kevin had mixed for me. As usual, every ceiling was flat white, every wall was flat rice paper, and every piece of trim was semi-gloss rice paper. I would be putting new carpeting in the living room and bedrooms, and new linoleum in the kitchen. The rest of the floors I would paint with a dark brown, semi-gloss floor paint.

I stacked the boxes of paint on a hand truck and wheeled them up to Edgar's apartment. When I dropped one of the paint boxes on the dining room floor, one of the floorboards moved. I picked the box back up a few inches and let it drop again. The floorboard shook. *I'll have to nail that back down*, I thought. I slid the box to the side, figuring I would go ahead and renail it now, so I wouldn't forget.

I went to my toolbox and grabbed my hammer and a couple finish nails. When I returned to the floorboard, I got down on my knees. I stuck my fingertips between the two pieces of wood, and lifted. The floorboard came up, revealing a metal box that rested between the floor joists. The box was about fourteen inches by sixteen inches, and around eight inches deep. I pulled out the box, set it on the floor next to me, and opened the lid. Inside was a lot of cash. I instinctively looked around the room to make sure no one else was there. I wanted to start counting but was afraid someone might walk in.

I hurried down the hall to the door, locked it, and ran back to the box. I took out some bills and started counting; they were all hundreds. It took me about twenty-five minutes to count the money. When I had finished, the total came to $218,000. *Holy cow*, I thought. *Motive*.

Someone jiggled the doorknob, and then knocked. I frantically started shoving money back into the box. It seemed like there was a lot more than I had taken out. It was like having a pile of dirt left over after refilling a hole. I started shoving the bills into the space between the joists and then jammed the box in behind them. I replaced the floorboard, picked up my hammer and nails, and ran for the door, tossing my hammer on the countertop as I ran by.

"Hey," I said, when I opened the door. Rance and a familiar-looking young man in his twenties stood before me. I couldn't place him.

"What's the matter?" Rance asked.

"The matter?" I replied. "Why do you ask?"

"You're out of breath and your face is all red."

"You look like you just got caught pounding one off, dude," said the twenty-something. He grinned and looked to Rance for approval of his rapier wit. Rance just shook his head. The smile quickly left the kid's face.

"You'll have to excuse him," Rance said apologetically. "My sister's kid. He's an idiot."

The kid snickered as though he thought Rance was joking.

"Good one," I said to the kid.

"Donny, this is Mr. Langley."

We shook hands, and Donny told me that it was nice to meet me; I said the same. He asked me if he knew me from somewhere, that I looked familiar to him. I told him I didn't think so.

I turned and went back down the hall; Rance and Donny followed me. Donny stopped at each of the two bedrooms and peered inside. "Pretty nice," he said.

I walked into the kitchen and leaned against the sink. I folded my arms across my chest.

Donny and Rance walked from the kitchen to the dining room, and into the living room.

"Pretty nice," Donny said again. "How much."

"You'll have to ask Kevin," I said.

"He said you could have it for fifteen hundred a month," said Rance.

"Eesh," Donny responded. "That's kinda high. I'll probably need a roommate."

"I thought you said you had someone," Rance said.

"That fell through," said Donny.

"Then why are we here?"

"I know a couple other guys looking for a place," Donny assured him. "When's it gonna be ready?"

"Three or four weeks," I said.

"He doesn't work on Mondays or Fridays," Rance explained.

"Must be nice," said Donny.

Rance walked back across the dining room. The floorboard creaked and shifted beneath him. "Got a loose floorboard here," he said. "Someone could twist an ankle."

"Yeah, I saw that," I said. "A couple finish nails will fix it."

After Donny was done with his inspection, Rance asked, "Well, what do you think?"

"I'll think it over," Donny said.

"Okay then," I said, trying to give them the idea that I was busy and wanted badly to get back to work.

"Why did the previous tenant move out?" Donny asked.

Rance and I looked at each other.

"He moved into something smaller," Rance said.

"Yeah, a lot smaller," I added.

Rance shot me a look. "Let's get out of Rex's hair," he said. They went down the hall to the door. I locked it behind them and ran back to the loose floor board. It took me a few minutes, but I got all the cash back neatly into the lockbox. I tucked it under my arm, and headed for the elevator.

Just as the elevator doors were about to close, I hear the words to "Tiptoe Through the Tulips" echo through the hall. I shoved my arm through the opening, halting the closure and reopening the doors. I stepped off the elevator and listened as a man sang. He didn't know all the words, and hummed the parts he didn't know. It was coming from the other end of the hall. I put my ear up to Maude's door. It wasn't coming from here apartment. I walked down the hall to the next apartment and put my ear up against that door. The words were coming from inside. I knocked on the door. Sam Fuller answered.

"Hi, Rex," he said. "What's up?"

"Was that you singing?" I asked.

Sam grinned. "Yeah. Why?" He cocked his head suspiciously.

"What made you sing it?"

"Um … are you okay, Rex?" he asked.

"Yeah, Sam, I'm fine. I was just wondering: of all the songs in the world, why would you be singing that one?"

"Oh, you know. One of those earworms, I guess. Like when you hear someone singing 'John Jacob Jingleheimer Schmidt' and you can't get it out of your head."

"Did you hear someone singing 'Tiptoe Through the Tulips,' Sam?"

"I may have."

"Think, Sam," I urged. "It's important."

Sam stared at me like I had two heads. "The other night. I was in bed and I heard someone out here in the hall singing it."

"What night, Sam?"

Sam thought for a second. "I think it was two Sundays ago."

I did some quick mental arithmetic. That would have been the night before I found Edgar's dead body.

"You think, or you're sure?"

"Well, I know it was a Sunday night because I was laying there in bed watching *Madam Secretary*, and it wasn't this week, because this week was a repeat. You ever watch that *Madam Secre—*"

"Thanks, Sam. I gotta go."

"You take care, Rex," Sam called out, as I ran back down the hall.

When I arrived at my house, Chester and Ho were sitting in their driveway having an afternoon cocktail. I climbed out of my truck and Chester raised his glass into the air.

"Howdy neighbor," Chester called out.

"Hey, guys," I hollered back.

"Watcha got in the box there?" Chester asked.

"Two-hundred and eighteen thousand dollars," I shouted.

Chester and Ho chuckled.

"You're crazy," Ho hollered.

You got that right, I thought.

Chapter Twenty-Three

"You stole over two hundred thousand dollars!" Gayle hollered.

The tin lockbox sat open on the dining room table in front of Gayle and me.

"*Shh*," I said. "Not so loud. I didn't steal it. I just brought it home to show you. It's motive."

"You could have just told me about it."

"Would you have believed me?"

"Yes. But what makes you think it is motive?"

I was flushed with excitement. "Think about it," I said. "Someone knew Edgar had this money, and that someone wanted it. They went to his apartment to get it. He wouldn't tell them where it was, so they killed him."

"Who's they? Who would know Edgar had the money?"

"His brother."

"I thought you said his brother lived in South Carolina."

"He does."

"Then how did he get down here, kill his brother, and then get back to South Carolina? Didn't Rance tell you he didn't have a car to get to the funeral?"

"I don't know, but Sam Fuller said he heard someone in the hall singing 'Tiptoe Through the Tulips' the night Edgar was killed. Maybe he borrowed a car. Maybe he's lying and he does have a car."

Gayle threw up her arms. "Well, that's it. Case closed. Who the hell is Sam Fuller?"

"He lives over the hardware store."

"And what about 'Tiptoe Through the Tulips'?"

"You know, the song by Tiny Tim."

"I know the song."

"Maude said that Everette always walked around singing it."

"Then maybe he wasn't really in South Carolina when Rance spoke to him."

"Right!"

Gayle chuckled. "Or it may not have even been Edgar's money. He may not even have known it was there. Maybe it was put there before he ever moved in. Maybe Edgar just tried to change a light bulb, and the chair broke. A lot of people know the song 'Tiptoe Through the Tulips.'"

I sighed. "Yeah, maybe."

We stood there staring at the money for a few more seconds. "What should we do with it?" I asked Gayle.

"*We*? There's no we here. I have nothing to do with this."

"Then what should *I* do with it?"

"You have to take it to Detective Rance."

"Or …" I said, finger pointing skyward.

Gayle interrupted my aha moment. "Or what?" she demanded impatiently.

"We get a hold of Edgar's brother and see if he knows anything about the money."

"How do we find that out?"

"We tell him we found something under the floor boards and wondered if it was his."

"I doubt he's going to admit it."

"Let's just see what happens," I said.

Gayle threw up her hands in surrender. "Whatever," she said. "You do what you want. I'm jumping in the shower."

"You want me to come in with you?"

"No."

"I'll give you fifty thousand dollars."

"It ain't yours to give."

I watched Gayle wiggle down the hall in her tight white capris, and when she turned into the bedroom out of sight, I pulled out my cell phone.

"Rance," he answered.

Damn, that's cool. "Hey, it's Rex."

"What now?"

"Just wondering if you could get me Everette Hayes' phone number."

"Edgar's brother?"

"Yeah."

"What do you need that for?"

"Kevin wants me to give him a call and see if he can get down here to pick up Edgar's personal belongings."

"He told me he didn't own a car, so I don't know how he would get down here."

"Kevin said he would pay to have the boxes shipped to Everette if he wanted, just to get them out of storage."

"Hold on," Rance said. "I got the number here somewhere."

It was a good thirty seconds before Rance came back on the line and gave me the phone number. I jotted it down in pen on the palm of my hand, thanked him, and hung up. *That was easy*, I thought. I entered the phone number and name into my contacts and slid the cell back into the front pocket of my cargo shorts.

I grabbed a beer out of the fridge and walked out to the garage. I figured I would check on the Rays and see how they were doing in their second game in the series with the damn Yankees.

"Hey, Rex," Glenn said, when I opened the door that led from the living room to the garage. He held up a bottle of LandShark. He was sitting on the couch watching the game. "I'm hidin' from the old lady."

"Where'd you get the beer?" I asked.

"Chester's fridge. I got a key."

"They're not home?"

"I wouldn't have needed my key if they were home. Keep with the story, Rex."

"Sorry."

Have a seat, pal. "Top of the fifth, all tied up."

"Thanks for the offer, Glenn. I think I will have a seat on my own couch."

Gayle opened the door about forty-five minutes later and stuck her head into the garage. "Hey," she said.

Glenn put up a hand. "*Shh.*"

Gayle gave me one of those *Jerry Springer Show*, "*oh no he di'-int*" looks.

Glenn quickly apologized. "Sorry, Gayle. It's bottom of the ninth and still tied up. We got two men on and Wendle's coming to the plate."

Gayle smiled. "I'll let it go this time, Glenn."

Glenn and I were on the edge of our seats as the count climbed to three and two. Gayle sat down beside me. Wendle fouled one into the bleachers, and then another down the third baseline. Glenn was biting his nails. The pitch was a fastball right down the middle. Wendle swung. The thwack of the bat brought the crowd to its feet.

"Yes!" the three of us shouted. It was a game ending, walk-off triple.

"Nice!" said Glenn. He turned to Gayle. "What did you need, honey?"

"Yeah, snookums," I joked. "What did you need?"

"Did you get a hold of Detective Rance?" Gayle asked.

"Yeah," I replied. "He gave me Everette's number. I'll call in a few minutes."

Glenn set the empty LandShark bottle on the coffee table and stood up. "Welp," he said, stretching his arms over his head. "I better get going. Might still be able to get in a nap before bedtime."

We watched as Glenn went out through the screen door and down the driveway toward his house.

"Call now," Gayle said.

"What should I say to him?"

"Tell him you found something in the apartment and if he can describe it, he can have it."

I laughed. "Sounds too obvious."

"Whatever you say, it has to be obvious enough for him to know what you're talking about."

"That's true," I agreed. "Especially if he's as wacky as his brother."

"Let's assume he is."

"How about if I tell him I found a metal lock box under the floorboards with three hundred bucks inside."

"Oh, that's good. Three hundred might be enough to get him down here, especially if he knows there's supposed to be a lot more."

"What if he has to take a bus? Will three hundred bucks be worth it?"

"Make it four hundred."

"Okay." I grabbed my cell and dialed the number Rance had given me.

"Hello?" a man answered.

"Good evening," I said. "I'm trying to reach a gentleman by the name of Everette Hayes."

"Watchoo be wont'n wit 'im?" the man asked. I knew right away it was Edgar's brother. His crazy accent was identical.

"I'm doing some work in his late brother's apartment, and there's a few personal items I boxed up. I was wondering if Everette wanted them."

"Whut kinda items?"

"Is this Everette?" I asked.

"You gots ta speak up. I don't hear too well."

"Is this Everette?" I was shouting like Garrett Morris on the old "News for the Hard of Hearing' segment on *Saturday Night Live*.

"Dis be him," Everette said. "Whut kinda items ya be talkin' 'bout."

"Comic books, trophies, a few other things, and I found a metal lock box under the floorboards with four hundred dollars in it."

"How much?"

"Four hundred."

"Whut?"

"Four hundred!"

"That's all they be, four hundred?"

"Yup."

"You count it?"

"Yup."

"And that's all they be?"

"Yup."

"Where dat box now?"

"It's still at the apartment."

"Whut's dat?"

"I have it at the apartment!" I Shouted. Gayle stuck her fingers in her ears.

"Da money still in dare?"

"Yeah."

"You tell da *po*-lice 'bout dat money?"

"No. Why would I tell the police?"

"No reason. I'll be dare tomorry afternoon to pick up dat money."

"What about the other stuff?"

Um … yeah I get dat too."

Everette hung up.

I turned to Gayle. "He be here tomorry afternoon," I said, mocking Everette.

"Whut?" Gayle asked, playing along.

"Tomorry," I shouted.

"Tomorry?" she asked.

"Tomorry."

We both chuckled.

Chapter Twenty-Four

I went to work at the usual time Thursday morning. Gayle said she would be done with work by two and would come over to the apartment in case I needed back up. We were becoming a regular Jonathan and Jennifer Hart. Except I wasn't nearly as suave and good-looking as Robert Wagner.

I stopped into the hardware store first, like I did most mornings before going upstairs. Kevin and Christine stood at the checkout counter. Christine was cashing out some guy, and Kevin was explaining to another guy why his lawnmower wasn't repaired yet.

I waited patiently until the guy finally left. "Did you call to have that dumpster picked up?" I asked.

"Not yet," Kevin, the procrastinator, replied.

"You know they charge you by the day after the first five days."

"They do?"

"Yeah. You want me to call?"

"No. I'll call."

"Sure you will."

"You finished up there yet?" Kevin asked.

Kevin always asks me if I'm finished yet. He asks me every day, from the day I start a project, until the day I actually finish the project. I never know if he's busting my balls, or if he really thinks there's a chance I might complete a four-week project in one day.

"Yeah," I replied. "All finished. Someone can move in tomorrow." That's how I always answer when he asks me if I'm finished. "Has the drain leaked since I fixed it?"

"No."

"I see the bucket is still sitting there. I thought maybe it was leaking again."

"I just forgot to move it."

"I'll get it."

I walked down the hardware aisle and picked up the bucket. It was empty, which meant someone had emptied it, and then put it back under a pipe that no longer leaked. Better to be safe than sorry, I guess. I tossed the bucket into the utility room at the end of the aisle and walked back to the front of the store.

"I'm heading upstairs," I said.

"Have fun," said Christine.

"You know it," I replied.

I walked down the hall and rode the elevator up to the second floor. When I got to Edgar's door, it was already unlocked. I turned the knob and went inside. As I went in, I checked the strike plate and cylinder as Gayle had told me. There was no damage. Maybe I forgot to lock up. Not too smart with all my tools inside.

When I got to the dining room the first thing I noticed was that the loose floorboard had been removed and was lying next to the opening. I took out my cell phone and called downstairs.

"Kevin, it's Rex."

"Yeah?"

"Were you in Edgar's apartment last night or this morning?"

"No. I try never to go up there."

"Strange. The door was unlocked."

"You probably forgot to lock it."

"Yeah. Prob'ly." I hung up the cell and slipped it into my back pocket.

I looked around one more time and shrugged it off. I knew I had walked out of empty apartments before without locking them.

I decided to start painting the ceilings, so I grabbed a can of flat white, and one of the disposable paint trays I had brought up from the store. I crouched down next to the can and popped off the cover with a flathead screwdriver.

"Where's mah money?" someone behind me asked.

I froze. *Oh shit*.

"Turn yerself around," said the voice.

There was a part of me hoping it was Rance playing a joke on me to get even for spooking him the other day, but I knew it wasn't. The voice was familiar and unmistakable.

I slowly turned around to see a man holding a revolver. The poor devil looked a lot like Edgar, holding a revolver. I put up my hands, even though he didn't ask me to.

"Don't do anything stupid," I said. I rose up with my hands still in the air.

"I'z gonna say da same thing ta you."

"You must be Everette."

"How's dat?"

"You must be Everette," I repeated, a little louder.

"And you must be da dumb bastert's got my money. Where it be?"

"It's not here," I explained. "I have it at my house."

I heard the door open. Everette didn't seem to notice.

"That's an awful big gun you have there, Everette," I said loudly. I hoped Everette would appreciate me speaking a little louder, but mostly I hoped whoever came in heard me.

Everette glanced down and admired his weapon. "Dis be one ah doze .44 Mangnims," he boasted. "Jest like da one dat Clint Eastman gots."

"Eastwood," I corrected.

"How's dat?"

"It's Clint Eastwood."

"Dat's whut I say."

"Where'd you get a gun like that?" I yelled.

"Gots dis wit my half da money."

"Your half?" I asked. "Where did you and Edgar get all that money?"

Everette grinned. He had about three more teeth than his brother, but they were just as black. "From dat ol' lady Edgar work fer, doin' odd jobs. Lady by the name of Barnum"

"You stole it?"

"No!" Everette shot back. "We jus' taked it. She din't need it anymer."

"Why didn't she need it anymore?"

"She's daid."

"How'd she die?"

I heard a floorboard in the hall creak. I didn't look away from Everette.

"She fell down her stairs while Edgar was workin' dere. He callt me on da phone and I went over. Dat poor ol' lady was layin' at da bottom ah doze stairs. She was all broked. I bent down and put my hand over her nose and mouth till she quit twitchin'. Put 'er out 'er miz' ry. Den me an Edgar looked around dat house and fount da money. Edgar'd seen her hidin' place when he'd done jobs of work at her place. He didn' wan' to take it but I talked him inter it."

"And you each took half," I surmised.

Edgar grinned toothlessly. "Dat's right. We made a pact tah keep quiet 'bout da money. I moved up to South Caroline-y where ah knowed I could live high on da hog wedout raesen' 'specions. Tol' ever'body ah'd inherited dat money from my daddy. Dey whutn't any da weser."

"So you spent all your loot." obviously not on dental work or hearing aids. "On what?"

"Soaked mahself in whisky and whores. Gambled some. And when I call up ol' Edgar, tellin' him I'z broked, he say he never spend any ah his. But he say I can't have none. Edgar always be crazy. Jest squirreled all dat money away rather than makin' hisself happy wid it. So I decided ah'd make *mahself* happy wid it."

"So you came here to get it and killed him."

"Dat's also right. And I'm a gonna kill you too iffin you don't get dat money for me."

"Freeze!" Rance shouted, as he stepped into the doorway.

Everette spun around and fired a round into the doorjamb, a shower of splinters blinding Rance for half a second. The big Magnum's kick had sent Everette reeling. The little man was just leveling the gun when Rance's shot struck him in the chest.

Everette stumbled back and dropped. He tried to raise his gun again as he sat there, but he didn't have the strength. The hole in his chest looked like a cannon ball had gone through it. He slumped forward, and then tipped over, hitting the side of his head on the wooden floor. He was dead, but his eyes were open. It looked like he was staring at the hole in the floorboards where Edgar had kept the metal lockbox.

"Thank you," I said.

Rance walked to Everett's body and kicked the revolver to the other side of the room, and then jammed his own weapon back into his shoulder holster. "Don't mention it," he said.

"Did you hear all that?" I asked.

"Are you kidding? With all that yelling you were doing?"

"I meant Everette's confession."

"Yeah, I heard."

"We make quite a team."

"We don't make a team at all." Rance pulled out his cell and dialed.

"I was talking about me and Gayle," I said. "Oh! Now I remember." I smacked my forehead with the palm of my hand.

"Remember what?"

"Where I saw your nephew before. Him and a friend were at Dairy Queen last week and they kept staring at my wife's tits."

Rance shook his head. "Swell."

Chapter Twenty-Five

Later that afternoon I handed the cash over to Detective Rance and he told me that I was an asshole. Then he reminded me that the body count around me was now at two. How he thinks Everette's death was my fault is beyond me. I was just trying to help out.

Old Lady Barnum's relatives had two hundred and eighteen grand coming their way; they'd be happy about that. I didn't know how happy they would be finding out her death was a homicide and not an accident. It was coming to light that Mrs. Barnum was an eccentric character whose modest lifestyle masked her wealth. She had given Edgar—and other poor souls in similar circumstances—odd jobs purely out of the goodness of her heart. And look where it got her.

Gayle and I lay in bed staring up through the slowly spinning ceiling fan discussing the case we had just solved. She wasn't as proud of herself as I was proud of myself. I figured it was because she had solved cases before. I, on the other hand, was new to the feeling.

"I thought it was odd that Rance didn't thank us for our help," I mentioned.

"Are you really?" Gayle asked.

"I guess not."

I changed the subject. "Gayle," I said, "do you think Edgar and Everette were ... well, evil?"

"Hmm, let me see. Edgar was an incorrigible hoarder, but I don't think he was evil. Remember, he didn't want to take Barnum's money, and he never spent his share, he just, well, hoarded it, like everything else. I imagine he felt remorse for Mrs. Barnum's death. I don't think Everette was evil either—at first. Everette actually thought he was putting poor Mrs. Barnum out of her misery by asphyxiating her, rather than summoning help. I think all that money corrupted him, to the point he thought nothing of killing his brother when he ran out of his ill-gotten booty. No, they weren't evil. But they were definitely more than a little off.

"Is that your official evaluation of the case?"

"Yes. G'night."

"G'night."

We drifted off to sleep, me dreaming of catching criminals and Gayle dreaming about whatever she dreams about; me, probably.

Sometime around three in the morning something awakened me; a clunk or a bump. I don't know, I was sleeping. I lay there with my eyes open staring at the wall. This was usually the point where Gayle jabbed me in the ribs and said, "Did you hear that noise?" I thought I heard someone whisper. I turned to wake up Gayle. The blankets on her side were pulled back and she was gone. Her nightstand drawer was open. *Shit!*

I swung my legs over the edge of the bed, opened my nightstand drawer, and grabbed my 9mm. I was trying to be as quiet as possible. I tiptoed down the hall, singing "Tiptoe Through the Tulips" in my head. *Goddamn song*, I thought.

When I was halfway down the hall I saw Beau Haskell standing in the darkness, right next to his brother's bloodstain. He said, "Don't do this, Bobby Joe. You said we was just gonna scare them."

I couldn't see Bobby Joe but I heard him whisper back, "Shut up. We gotta teach these people a lesson."

I moved to the other wall and pressed my back up against it. I sidestepped a few feet further, keeping my back against the wall, and my gun in both hands. I gently removed the safety. There was no way to see into the living room without Beau seeing me.

I stepped from the hall, my weapon trained on Beau. It startled him. He flinched.

"Don't move," I said.

Gayle was on her back on the living room floor. Bobby Joe Haskell was on his knees, straddling her. His pants were unbuttoned and his fly was unzipped.

Gayle's pajama top was torn and she was trying her best to cover her breasts with her left arm.

Bobby Joe had her right arm pinned to the floor, and held Gayle's .38 in his right hand. When he heard me he put the gun to Gayle's forehead and said, "Drop the gun, asshole."

"You drop yours," I replied.

Bobby Joe pulled back the hammer. I heard the awful sound of it clicking into place.

"Just do what he says, Langley," said Beau.

"Don't you put down that gun, Rex!" Gayle screamed. She looked more angry than scared.

"Shut up, bitch!" Bobby Joe hollered.

"Please put down the gun, Langley," Beau pleaded. "He'll kill her."

"Don't do it, Rex!" Gayle shouted.

"Shut up!" Bobby Joe yelled. He turned his gun on me and Gayle brought up her knee into his crotch.

Bobby Joe fell forward and fired, hitting Beau in the shoulder.

I jumped behind the couch as Bobby Joe fired again. I came up and Gayle was wrestling Bobby Joe for the weapon. Bobby Joe pulled the trigger again, the bullet hitting the floor to Gayle's left, missing her head by inches.

I rested my forearms on the back of the couch, aimed, took a deep breath, and fired.

The right side of Bobby Joe's head exploded, sending blood, brains, and shards of skull across the room. Bobby Joe fell dead on his side on the carpeting.

I returned my attention to Beau Haskell.

"Please," he said, "please don't shoot."

"Get on your knees," I ordered.

Beau did as he was told.

Gayle was up and moving across the room. Covering her breasts was of no importance to her now. I watched as she stopped in front of Beau, planted both feet, and screamed. She brought up her right foot, hitting Beau under the chin. His head snapped back violently, and he was out cold on his back.

Gayle turned and ran into my arms. She sobbed, and I squeezed her hard.

When Gayle had stopped shaking, I brought her into the bedroom and she sat down on the bed. I fetched her robe and she put it on over the ripped top.

"Stay here," I said. I walked back down the hall. Beau was still unconscious, and Bobby Joe was still dead. I got out my cell phone and dialed.

"Rance," he answered, and cleared the sleep from his throat.

"Hey, pal, it's me," I said.

"We ain't pals," he replied. "What now?"

"Remember earlier today when my body count was at two?"

"Yeah."

"I need my card punched again."

The End

Coming Soon:

We Call it Suicide

A Dunquin Cove Story

High Maintenance

From Fernandina Beach Mysteries

Excited About Nothing

Jake Stellar Series

ALSO BY RODNEY RIESEL

From the Tales of Dan Coast Series
Sleeping Dogs Lie
Ocean Floors
The Coast of Christmas Past
Ship of Fools
Double Trouble
Most Likely to Die
Deadly Moves
On the Wagon
No Enemies Here

Jake Stellar Series
North Murder Beach
Beach Shoot
When Death Returns
The Obedience of Fools
Dead in the Water

The Dunquin Cove Series
The Man in Room Number Four
Return to Dunquin Cove

Sunrise City Series
Sunrise City
Sunrise City 2: From Bad to Worse
Never Strikes Twice

From Here to There: A Collection of Short Stories

Made in the USA
San Bernardino, CA
28 November 2019